7/21 ✓

Withdrawn

FREEFALL
SUMMER

FREEFALL SUMMER

TRACY BARRETT

Charlesbridge
TEEN

Published by Charlesbridge
85 Main Street
Watertown, MA 02472
(617) 926-0329
www.charlesbridge.com

Library of Congress Cataloging-in-Publication Data:
Names: Barrett, Tracy, 1955- author.
Title: Freefall summer / Tracy Barrett.
Description: Watertown, MA : Charlesbridge, [2018] | Summary: When she was six years
old Carys "Clancy" Edwards's mother died in a skydiving accident and in the ten years
since her father has refused to even let her think about skydiving, despite the fact that it
is his business--but Clancy is now sixteen and she is beginning to think that it is time to
break out of the protective cocoon her father has woven around her.
Identifiers: LCCN 2017003933 (print) | LCCN 2017021900 (ebook) |
ISBN 9781632896414 (ebook) | ISBN 9781580898010 (reinforced for library use)
Subjects: LCSH: Skydiving—Juvenile fiction. | Fathers and daughters—Juvenile fiction.
| Single-parent families—Juvenile fiction. | CYAC: Skydiving—Fiction. | Fathers and
daughters—Fiction. | Single-parent families—Fiction. | LCGFT: Bildungsromans.
Classification: LCC PZ7.B275355 (ebook) | LCC PZ7.B275355 My 2018 (print) |
DDC 813.54 [Fic] —dc23
LC record available at https://lccn.loc.gov/2017003933

Printed in the United States of America
(hc) 10 9 8 7 6 5 4 3 2 1

Display type set in Breakfast Burrito by David Kerkhoff
Text type set in Adobe Caslon Pro
Printed by Berryville Graphics in Berryville, Virginia, USA
Production supervision by Brian G. Walker
Designed by Sarah Richards Taylor

For Greg, of course

Whuffo: Someone who hasn't made a skydive (yet), especially a spectator. Supposedly derives from "*What for* do you jump out of a perfectly good airplane?"

—*The Whuffo's Guide to Skydiving*

1

When my dad likes a woman, he always invites her over to dinner for Beef Stroganoff, and I have to be there. "It's better to let her see how it really is around here," he says, including the fact that he has a sixteen-year-old daughter. It's okay if my boyfriend, Theo, or one of my friends, even Cory with the tattoos circling his neck, comes over too. Dad says that if she can't see past Cory's tattoos, she's too closed-minded for him. That kind of thing is why my friends say my dad is cool. They'd think he was cool even if tattoos bothered him, though. Most of them are awestruck by him, and the fact that he makes their parents a bit nervous doesn't hurt.

After dinner my dad puts on a "family video." It starts with a four-year-old girl—me—at the drop zone, wearing a pink jumpsuit and a backpack that my dad modified to look like a parachute container. I'm wearing little military-looking jump boots, like skydivers used to wear. Most of the time my dad's date says something like, "Aw, she's so cute!" And I was. I had a saddle of freckles over my nose, and my pigtails were so blond they were almost white, not whatever color my hair is now—something between blond and light brown. Anyway, four-year-old me swaggers around like I own the place. The camera shakes because my mom, who's filming, is trying not to laugh.

First-jump students stand silently at the fence watching canopies open and jumpers land. They know that soon they'll be on board the Caravan, then they'll climb to altitude, and, one by one, they'll jump out attached to my dad or one of the instructors who work for him (who will keep them stable and open the canopy and make sure they land in the right place, not hung up in a tree or sizzling on power lines). Then, one by one, they'll land and shout "Woo-hoo!" and say that it was awesome and swear they're coming back the next weekend. And then they'll drive home and never make another jump.

I've seen the video so many times I feel like I remember that day. I strut up and down the line looking at the first jumpers. Two girls ask me my name and how old I am, trying to pretend they aren't terrified. I ignore them and go up to the guy who looks the palest, the most like he's about to throw up, and I stare at him until he's obviously

2

uncomfortable. Then I ask in as spooky a voice as I can squeak out, "*Can you smell it?*"

The guy looks confused. "I don't smell anything."

I tilt my head and sniff. I ask a little louder, "Can you smell it?" The camera shakes again, and you hear a snort escape from my mom.

Someone finally says, "Smell what?"

Then I say, "Death!" I stomp my foot like I'm squashing a bug and shout, "WHOMP!"

I'm always curious how my dad's date will react to that. Usually, she giggles nervously. Sometimes she says something like, "Goodness!"

And my dad says, "I have no idea who taught her that. Not good for business." He sounds serious, but you can hear that he thinks it's funny.

But I know. I know who taught me that. And my dad does too; I remember when he got mad at my mom and told her she was scaring off customers.

After the "WHOMP!" the first part of the video ends because my mom cracked up so hard, she had to stop filming. The second part shows my dad doing formations in the air with his team the year they won the nationals, and then a world-record attempt he was in. That formation funneled right before the last person closed, but it was really pretty anyway.

Last comes a TV news report about my mom's team doing a demo jump into a rock concert at the university in Springfield. My mom's canopy opens with line twists, so she cuts away really low and goes back into freefall a heartbeat before her reserve opens. The crowd loves it. They scream while the reporter shouts about how my mom was mere seconds away from death and how they had all witnessed a miracle.

That's where the news report ends, but whoever sent it to my dad gave us the uncut version, which makes the reporter look really stupid. The guy asks my mom what she was thinking as she "plummeted to earth," and she says, "I was worrying I'd broken a fingernail." (She was messing with him—my mom's fingernails were as short as mine.) She takes her helmet off, and her short blond hair is plastered to her head with sweat, but even so, she is so beautiful that it's hard to look at her. The reporter keeps trying to get her to open up about how her life must have flashed before her eyes, and she finally says in this really condescending way, "Look, buddy, it happens. It's part of skydiving. You don't wet your pants every time someone runs a red light or cuts you off on the freeway, do you? Jumping is a lot safer than driving and a hell of a lot safer than keeping skydivers talking instead of letting them use their backstage passes. So run along." Then she actually pats him on the head and leaves him standing there with a red face, looking like he wants to cry.

Then Dad always pops the DVD out, and here's where the test comes in: each date gets a grade based on the first thing she says. He tells me her grade after she leaves. I've given up telling him that it's ridiculous to judge someone based on this one thing. My dad says that if a woman isn't okay with him being a jumper, there's not much point in seeing her again. Seeing how much time he spends at the drop zone, I guess that's reasonable. Kind of.

Most times, his date says he's crazy to jump. That earns her a D. He tells her he appreciates her honesty and doesn't try to convince her that skydiving is actually a lot safer than most people think. If he likes everything else about her, he might call her again. But he usually doesn't.

If she says, "I don't see why you'd jump out of a perfectly good airplane," which every single whuffo says to every single skydiver like it's the most original and witty thing they've ever heard, he'll find some excuse to end the date early. He won't even bother to give her one of the standard jumper responses ("Because the door was open" or "You've obviously never seen a jump plane"). That "perfectly good airplane" line gives her an F, and he'll never call her again.

If his date says something like, "That looks really cool," she passes with a B. She doesn't have to say that she's always wanted to jump—he has lots of whuffo friends, not to mention a daughter he hopes will be a permanent whuffo, and he'd be fine with a whuffo girlfriend as long as she doesn't mind that he spends every weekend at the DZ. But he doesn't like gonna-jumpers who talk about it and never do it, so if she does say she's always wanted to skydive, he tells her great, he'll put her out the next Saturday. If she backs out, her grade drops to a C. If she actually jumps, her grade goes up to an A, even if she hates it and says she'll never do it again. "At least she tried," he says on the rare occasions when this happens.

One thing that isn't on my dad's video is a shaky, over-exposed recording that lasts less than two minutes. I don't think he's ever seen it—he's not too good with computers.

One day I searched "jenna clancy last jump" on YouTube, and there it was. At first I couldn't watch it all the way through, but after a few tries I made it to the end. Then I slammed my computer lid shut, thinking in some weird way that I was trapping the video in there, and didn't go online again for days.

Every few months I get an itchy, anxious feeling, and I know I have to see it again. I wait until my dad's out of the house. He doesn't bother me when I'm in my room with the door closed, but somehow I would feel uncomfortable if I watched it with him around.

First, I always check how many views it's gotten. I don't read the comments—not after the first time, when people said things that I wished I hadn't seen about chicks skydiving and about how deep a crater she must have made.

Anyway, the recording starts with the four members of my mom's competition team exiting the plane. At first they're just little dots. They grow a bit larger, and you can see that they're practicing the routine for the nationals. The sky is so bright behind them that you can hardly see them joining into a star and then a donut and then more formations, so fast and precise it doesn't look like real people but like computer animation. It's beautiful, but it doesn't last long, because jumpers only get about a minute of freefall. They break apart and pull. One, two, three hot-pink canopies blossom against the blue Missouri sky.

My mom's best friend, Angie, is recording from the ground. She was on the demo team but wasn't great at formation skydiving, so another teammate, named Michelle, took her place for formation, which didn't leave Angie much to do while the competition team was practicing. On the video she talks to someone you can't see, identifying who's who by how they fly their canopies. "There's Patsy . . . and Louisa . . . and Michelle." She doesn't sound worried at first as she says, "Now where's Jenna?" She sweeps the camera around and stops at a black dot against the brilliant blue that I know is my mom, but her canopy isn't open. Instead, there's a lumpy, misshapen thing flapping behind her.

"That's Jenna." Uncertainty and tension creep into Angie's voice. "She's—I can't tell—it looks like—it's a bag lock." And that's what it is: the canopy is stuck partway out of its container. My mom flips over on her back. This should pull the canopy out, but it doesn't. Then she flips again so she's belly-down and stable, but the canopy hasn't budged. Angie starts calling, "Oh God, Jenna, cut it away! Cut away, Jenna!" Another voice nearby yells the same thing, and even though my mom is obviously too far away to hear them, that's exactly what she does, as though she's following their instructions. She pulls the cutaway handle to release the risers from her rig, and for a second it looks like everything will be okay, but the main canopy doesn't fly away like it should. It remains hung up, half in the bag and half out of it. My mom tries to clear it, but she doesn't have much time, and then the automatic activation device on her reserve canopy deploys. But just at that moment the main canopy finally works itself free, and the reserve flies right up into it and catches its lines, tangling the two of them together.

The two canopies wrap up into a long, swirling streamer—the pink main and the white reserve twisted together like some gigantic, deadly candy cane—and my mom is spinning under it. She's so low that you can see her twirling as she jerks and tugs on the lines to free the reserve from the mess of the main. Angie's screaming and she must be running, because everything gets bumpy and shaky. Then she drops the camera, and all you can see is grass, and all you can hear is screaming and crying.

And then it ends.

2

My dad had been seeing Elise for a few weeks before she came over for Stroganoff night. I had met her before and she seemed nice enough, but I knew better than to get to know one of my dad's dates and maybe start to like her until after the video test. She was nice-enough looking too. Her brown hair was long and kind of wild, despite the combs and things she used in an attempt to tame it. I could tell it was colored but it looked pretty natural, and she was a little overweight. (Not like my mom, who had been thin, like me. To be fair, my mom was only twenty-six when she died, and maybe by now she would have put on some weight too.)

Anyway, Elise was easy to talk to at dinner and was

even kind of funny, and she passed the video test afterward. Nothing about a "perfectly good airplane" crossed her lips. When she said she'd like to make a jump, her grade stood at a provisional B. *Just saying you're going to jump is like doing a dirt dive,* I thought. *You can do fine when nothing's at stake, but you never know what will happen until you're actually standing in the door of the plane.*

I wondered if Elise would actually do it and wind up with an A. It had been a while since my dad had seen a woman more than a few times, at least as far as I knew.

She did show up at the drop zone the next Saturday. My dad offered to put her out on a static line. Elise asked what that was. He told her it was like what soldiers use, where they're attached to a cord that pulls the parachute open right after they exit. She said, "No, thanks. I don't want to go out that door by myself!" I wasn't surprised; none of the Stroganoff ladies have ever accepted the static-line offer, which I think would get them an A+.

He didn't try to convince her, even though he always says that making a jump while tethered to someone else takes half the fun out of it. All he said was, "That's fine. I'll send you out with Leon."

We were in the hangar, which is made of corrugated metal and gets really, really hot in the summer and freezing cold in the winter. I was in the back of the cavernous space, packing student rigs. I had been packing ever since I turned sixteen the spring before, which was okay as long as a certified rigger was around to supervise me. My dad paid me five dollars per standard pack job, ten dollars for a tandem rig.

Sometimes fun jumpers would pay me to pack for them, and they almost always gave me a tip on top of the packing fee, mostly because I'd known a lot of them since I was born.

I glanced at my dad as he strapped Elise into a harness. She didn't giggle or say anything stupid while he adjusted the chest straps. She said "Ow" once, but that was okay; he had to know if he'd gotten it too tight. When she was all rigged up, Dad took her into the office, where Cynthia was working the manifest, to get her on a load. Elise came back alone and stood in the doorway of the hangar, looking nervous. I shoved the canopy I was working on into its container and stowed the lines.

I earn less than some other packers because I'm always extra careful, and that makes me slow. Sometimes a jumper new to Skydive Knoxton—my dad's DZ—will tease me about it, asking if I'm crocheting or something. Someone always pulls them aside, and when I see them again I know by the way they avoid my eye that they've just learned about my mom. A part of me is relieved that they won't say anything more about it, a part of me is pissed that everybody has to know my private business, and a part of me wishes that for once, someone would ask *me* about it.

Leon came in and got Elise, and they went out to the plane. I didn't go out to watch. Sometimes I got twinges of resentment or envy when one of my dad's dates made a jump. If just once he would have said, "You know, Clancy, maybe I'm wrong. Maybe you could handle it. Why don't I put you out on your eighteenth birthday?" Instead, he encouraged women he hardly knew to make a jump.

Some of the regulars were packing in the hangar or hanging around waiting for the stream of students to die down. One group was dirt diving outside the door. The jumpers I knew came to say hi or waved at me when they arrived. Ripstop, the old, gray DZ cat, rubbed against my ankles. I bent down and scratched him between his raggedy ears. He purred. I picked him up and nuzzled him until he'd had enough and squirmed out of my grasp.

"I know how you feel, buddy," I said to him as he stalked away with his tail in the air, its tip twitching. At a certain point, you need your space.

Since Dad was running two planes, I kept busy. I listened to music, but I still heard the first plane take off. Pretty soon another engine revved, and then the first plane landed, and another group headed out. The jumpers from the first load came back into the hangar, whooping and laughing, so I had a new pile of rigs to pack. I stopped and stretched whenever I could, but my back was still getting sore from the way I had to stay bent over. I glanced at the clock and grimaced. I'd only been working an hour, even though it felt like all day.

Elise's load landed, and my dad came out of the office and stood in the doorway of the hangar. He grinned as she trotted up and threw her arms around him. "That was so much *fun!*" she almost shouted. "I was hardly scared at all." Her curly brown hair had escaped from its elastic, and her smile nearly split her face in two. She kept talking while he undid the straps and pulled the harness off her. Lots of students babble out of relief that the jump is done, but

Elise looked more excited than relieved, like she had really enjoyed it.

Then she called over to me, "I bet you can't *wait* until you're old enough to do this!"

The smile left my dad's face, and he looked like someone had punched him in the stomach. Before I could come up with one of my stock answers, Elise's eyes widened and she covered her open mouth with one hand. "Oh, honey, I'm so sorry! I totally forgot . . ."

Totally forgot that your mother died right out there, only a few hundred yards from where I landed safe and sound five minutes ago. Totally forgot that you were here that day.

"It's okay," I said, falsely cheery. I didn't want her to feel bad that she had forgotten—adrenaline will do that to you. Plus, it's not like people avoided talking about jumping around me, which would be impossible at the DZ, anyway. *Don't say anything*, I silently begged my dad, but of course he had to "set the record straight," as he put it.

"Clancy isn't going to jump. She's not so good at thinking on her feet." He glanced at me, but I turned back to the packing table so he wouldn't see my face, which I felt growing hot. "Jumping isn't the right sport for her. If she had to make a decision in a hurry . . ." He shook his head without finishing.

"Dad . . ." I swallowed the whiny tone. *I should just let it go*, I thought. When I turned eighteen it wouldn't be up to him. I'd be legal, and if I wanted to skydive and hang glide and bungee jump and get a tattoo, I'd do it. Maybe all of them on the same day.

I didn't say that, of course. I didn't want him passing out on the floor or sending me to a boarding school with bars on the windows, so I said as reasonably as I could, "You always say that, but when I ask you for examples of 'poor decision-making skills'"—I made air quotes with my fingers—"you can't ever give me any. If you—" I saw Elise trying to slip away from this family squabble, and I stopped. I bent back over the lines I was untangling so my dad wouldn't see my face. I knew he wasn't the only clueless parent in the world, but surely he'd know how humiliating it was to have Elise be a witness to how he treated me like a ditz.

"We'll talk about this another time," my dad said.

"Yeah, right," I muttered. I knew we wouldn't.

Rippy hopped up on the table and batted at the lines. I pushed him away and worked without speaking until I was sure my dad and Elise were gone.

I closed the last pack and glanced out the door. From the looks of the wind sock, it might get too breezy for students soon, maybe even for the fun jumpers. It was the weekend before the start of summer school at Clemens, and the college students had a whole summer's worth of money in their pockets and no homework to do yet. I hoped my dad would be able to put out at least one more load. That would mean four, maybe five pack jobs, just from student rigs. Every dollar I earned went into my savings so that I could eventually go away to college. There's nothing wrong with Clemens, but it was practically in my backyard, and I knew my dad would always find some excuse to drop in, even if he let me live in a dorm.

"And I'll become an archaeologist and go on digs in some country where no one's ever heard of skydiving," I grumbled to myself. Ha. Like such a country existed. I'd probably be in the rain forest digging up an arrowhead that proved that Amazonian Indians actually came from Scotland when some guy in a rig would land in front of me and say, "Aren't you Dave Edwards's kid?"

Cynthia's voice came crackling into the hangar, telling everyone that we were on a weather hold and only fun jumpers could go up—no students. The load that was already up landed, and the students trickled into the hangar. Rigs piled up next to me. The students trickled out again, laughing and talking, and then one of them turned back and called into the hangar, "Which one of you guys is Clancy?"

I suppressed a groan as I straightened up and looked at the student standing in the doorway. Right behind him stood Noel, who made a jack-o'-lantern grin at me behind the guy's back. He always thought it was funny to let people think I was a man.

"Clancy?" the guy asked. He looked at Buddy, who shook his head. He turned to Mad Jack, who shrugged.

I put the student out of his misery by raising my hand. "Here."

He looked at me warily, like he thought he would be providing the punch line to a joke. "I mean the Clancy who packed my parachute," he explained. "I want to thank him for saving my life." He sounded hyped up on adrenaline, and his ears were probably still stopped up, which would explain why he was so loud.

"I'm the Clancy who packed your parachute," I said. "And you're welcome."

Noel tossed his rig onto the pile and picked up his regular gear to join the group of fun jumpers that was forming outside the door. When I glanced up to find Noel's tandem rig, the student was still there. "Sorry." He sounded like he meant it. "It just didn't occur to me—I mean, I never thought—"

"It's okay. I know there aren't many girls called Clancy. It's really my middle name. And Noel likes doing that. He thinks he's a comedian." The guy looked sheepish and even blushed a little. "I'm a good packer even though I'm a girl, if that's what's bothering you. I know what I'm doing. I don't make parachutes or repair them or anything—I just pack them, and it's legal, even though—"

"Oh, I'm sure it's legal. And I'm sure you know what you're doing—it opened and everything."

He looked nice when he smiled. I noticed that he wasn't much taller than me, if at all, and had light brown hair and kind of gold-colored eyes. Long eyelashes. A nice face with a cleft chin. I realized I was staring and started on Noel's pack.

Leon came in carrying a rig and the student stuck out his hand at him. "Thanks again," he said. "It was awesome."

"You got the wrong guy." Leon tossed his rig next to the table and went out, leaving the student staring after him.

"That was Leon," I told him. "You jumped with Noel."

"But that guy looks just like—"

"Leon and Noel are identical twins," I said. "At least they look identical—same height, same receding hairline, same potbelly, same everything else. But actually, they're totally different. Leon's right-handed; Noel's a lefty. Leon is quiet; Noel never shuts up. Leon's gay; Noel's straight."

"Wow! It's kind of like they're mirror images, like their names."

I nodded, surprised that he noticed it so quickly. "They even part their hair on opposite sides. Their mom promised her father she'd name her first son Leon after him. Then when she had twins she named the first one Leon and the second one Noel so they'd both have his name, kind of."

"Good thing her dad wasn't named Bob."

It took me a moment to get it, and then I laughed. "Or Otto!"

"Or Pip. Or Asa."

"Asa?"

He shrugged. "It's a name." Then he blushed again. "My name's Denny. Dennis Rider, really, but nobody calls me Dennis except my grandmother."

"If you had a twin, the two of you would be Dennis Sinned," I said.

He smiled. "Never thought of that. Can't do much with Clancy, though—Clancy . . . " He wrote the letters in the air and acted like he was reading it. "Ycnalc."

"Sounds Klingon," I said. "My dad sometimes calls me C.C. That would work backward. My real first name is easier than Clancy, though. Backward, it's Syrac."

"Your real name is Carys?"

"It's Welsh, after my dad's mother," I said. "No one ever knows how to pronounce it, so when I started kindergarten, I told the teacher my name was Clancy. It was easier." That wasn't really true. I had still been Carys in kindergarten. It was in first grade that I changed it. And it wasn't because nobody could pronounce it. Lots of kids had names that made substitute teachers stumble, and they didn't switch to their middle names. No, it was because Clancy was my mom's last name, and I had practically nothing of hers left to me, just a few pictures. Her rings and the pearl necklace her grandmother had given her were technically mine, but they were in a safe-deposit box at the bank. My dad or Angie did something with the rig and costumes she had worn for demo jumps. I figured that since I had nothing else of hers, I could at least have her name.

The last student load landed, and the whoops and hollers started again, and the pile of rigs next to me grew. Denny's phone rang. He glanced at the screen and broke into a grin as he answered it. "F-bomb!"

F-bomb?

He hunched over his phone and turned away. "It was awesome! I can't wait till we do it together. You'll love it." He waved his free hand at me and walked out. I went back to my packing, and when I looked up again, he was sitting cross-legged against the wall, still talking. His face was shining, and even at that distance it looked like he had tears in his eyes.

Denny glanced up as though he felt me staring and smiled again. I quickly went back to my work, ignoring the little flutter in my belly, and the next time I looked toward the wall, he was gone.

I finally finished packing, and I was reading my *National*

Geographic in the beanbag chair when my phone beeped. Theo wanted to know if the weather was as bad at the DZ as it was in town. I felt a twinge of guilt that I hadn't even thought about him all day, or at least ever since I'd met Denny. That didn't mean anything, I told myself. It was just that it was a nice change having someone to talk to at the DZ. It made the time pass.

I looked out the hangar door, which was wide enough to allow a small aircraft to wheel in, and saw that the sky was gray. A piece of trash went skittering across the landing area, and I wondered how high the wind was. I hoisted myself up stiffly. How long had I been sitting there? It was hard to wrench my mind away from the ancient Aztecs and Incas I'd been reading about and focus on twenty-first-century Missouri.

In the office Cynthia was yawning and playing solitaire on the computer. She brightened when she saw me. "Tell Dave we need to close down," she said. "He won't listen to me."

"Where is he?"

She jerked her head in the direction of the lounge, behind the office.

I hesitated. "Is Elise with him?" I didn't want to interrupt anything.

She nodded. "Bunch of other people too." So that was okay.

In the lounge my dad sat on the saggy couch, with Elise next to him—not plastered against him, but being cozy. Leon and Noel were in armchairs, and Louisa and Patsy sat on folding chairs. A newish jumper named Zach, who had just come off student status, sat on the floor, teasing Ripstop with a length of cord.

They were telling shoulda-died stories. Skydivers never get tired of them. Louisa was in the middle of her best story, which I had heard zillions of times, about one day in the '90s when she'd been riding her motorcycle to a DZ in Arizona. She wore her rig on her back while she drove along the highway, and she locked it down so it wouldn't deploy by accident while she was on the road, which would probably be fatal. She got to the DZ just as a load was going up. She ran to the plane, forgetting about the condition of her rig, and when the plane turned on jump run, another jumper offered to give her a pin check.

"What's that?" Elise asked.

"Something jumpers used to do back in the day, when they jumped rounds and Para-Commanders," Zach said dismissively.

Elise looked blankly at Zach. "Old-style rigs," he explained. "They—"

"A pin check is something *some* jumpers still do," my dad broke in. "Including everyone at this DZ, on every load." He looked around to make sure they got his point, and then answered Elise. "The rig is on your back, which means you can't check yourself one last time to make sure everything is in place, so someone else on the load checks for you, and you do the same for them." He glared at Zach, who looked down at Ripstop as though the beaten-up old tomcat was suddenly interesting.

"Anyway," Louisa said hastily, "sure enough, the other

jumper saw that both my main and my reserve were locked down. The main never would have opened, and by the time I could have managed to unlock the reserve, it probably would have been too late."

"Wow." Zach shook his head. "You packed yourself a double malfunction."

Everyone digested that thought in silence. Even Rippy stopped playing with the string dangling from Zach's fingers and looked serious.

Angie says that after my mom died, it was a long time before anyone told shoulda-died stories around my dad, but it turned out he still liked hearing them and even telling them himself. I don't know why. Maybe it was because they're a reminder that a skydiving accident doesn't always have to end in death.

3

FACT: By far the primary cause of death and injury in skydiving is skydiver error, not equipment failure.

—*The Whuffo's Guide to Skydiving*

Elise caught sight of me in the doorway. She smiled and slid over, patting the cushion next to her. I shook my head. "I just need to talk to my dad."

Then everyone looked at me, and I wished I had told Cynthia that if she wanted to close up, she should be the one to ask my dad, not me. Too late now, and anyway, I would love to be home early enough on a Saturday to be able to do something with Theo.

"What is it, C.C.?" my dad asked.

"The wind isn't dropping and clouds are moving in."

Zach groaned. "My one day off this week!" He had

shown up at the DZ a few times in hospital scrubs, but whether he was a brain surgeon or an orderly or something in between, I didn't know.

"Let's see if it clears," my dad said. "The weather people don't know everything."

"*Dad.*"

"Just another hour."

"Oh, take her home," Noel said. "Back to that boyfriend."

"He's working," my dad said.

"No, he's not," I said. "Or he won't be for long. It's really cloudy in town, and they're going to close the pool." Theo hadn't exactly said that, but it was probably true.

In the end my dad said we'd wait until four o'clock and see. By then it was obvious that jumping was over for the day. Elise said good-bye to me and went outside with my dad, and in a minute her car pulled up to the parking lot exit. I watched as she turned onto the road and drove away. I wondered if she'd come back the next weekend. She was nice enough, and she wasn't trying to be a mother to me.

Leon and Noel were going to spend the night in their tents behind the hangar and hope for better weather on Sunday, and the rest of the jumpers loaded up their cars and left. Then my dad did some paperwork while I straightened out Cynthia's files, which were always a mess. I knew that if I nagged him, it wouldn't do anything except give him an excuse to lecture me, which would slow us down even more. We finally left just after five.

I'd gotten up before dawn since my dad likes to be on-site for the first load, so I slept most of the way back. It would be great to get home before the sun set for a change. My dad would have preferred to stay over Saturday night in the trailer we kept at the DZ, but even he could see how unfair it was to make me hang out at the DZ all weekend. When I was younger I used to go to summer camp—first for two weeks, then for a month, then for most of the summer—until I aged out. While I was away my dad would move to the DZ. Until I turned twelve or thirteen, it didn't bother me that I spent my weekends at the DZ with a lot of adults. But once I was old enough to have friends and a life of my own, I complained about staying there all weekend and seeing my friends only in school. My dad was reluctant to leave me with a babysitter, except Angie's daughter, Leanne, once or twice when he was in a bind.

Now that I was sixteen and obviously too old for a sitter, even according to my dad, people offered to drive me home when they were done jumping on Saturday and then bring me back again to the DZ on Sunday morning. But my dad still wouldn't let me stay in the house overnight by myself. That meant we had to get up really early on Sunday too, but at least I could go out on Saturday night.

I woke up when we were a few blocks from home and texted Theo. He didn't answer. As we pulled up to the house, I saw why: he was already on the porch, sitting on a step, with his long legs stretched out in front of him. His dark hair still glistened with pool water in the gray light coming from the cloudy sky, and his lean swimmer's build looked especially good.

He came down to the car to help me out. I'd given up

telling him that I didn't need help, and I let him open the door and offer me his hand, as though I was too fragile to struggle out of the seat by myself. Saint Theodore the Protector. I stifled a sigh of exasperation. Better to pick your battles, Angie always told me, and this wasn't very important. Plus, Theo liked being protective.

The air had cooled since we'd left the DZ, and a fresh breeze stirred my hair. Theo gave me a quick kiss, his chin stubble scraping my skin. I smiled up at him. He looked so good. In the dim light, his brown eyes were almost black, and I wished I could trace his jawline with my finger without my dad seeing.

My dad came around the car. "Anything in the trunk, sir?" Theo asked. He'd moved to Missouri from Birmingham, Alabama, the previous summer, but he still had a drawl that my best friend, Julia, said was the sexiest thing she'd ever heard.

"Nope." Dad shook Theo's hand. "We'll be going back first thing in the morning, so I left things there."

He wouldn't let me tease Theo for always shaking hands, for opening the door for me. He said it was refreshing to see a seventeen-year-old act like a gentleman. I knew he meant "refreshing as a boyfriend for my daughter" because he liked neck-tattoo Cory as just a friend for me, and he preferred adventurous girlfriends for himself. He also liked how Theo did man-stuff with him, such as when the refrigerator quit and the two of them fixed it together. If I offered to help, they'd act like it was cute and tell me they could handle it.

"Would it be all right if I took Clancy out to dinner tonight?" Theo asked him.

"Fine with me," he said.

"Um, fine with me too," I said pointedly. They both looked at me like they were surprised I could talk. I was kind of surprised too. I usually didn't say anything if they decided things for me, if I didn't care about whatever it was. If I did care, I'd probably say something after we weren't around my dad. Divide and conquer, after all. But I guess I was still irritated by the way my dad had spoken for me when Elise had said something about me making a jump, so I went on, "Isn't anybody going to ask whether I want to go out to dinner tonight?"

"There's nothing to eat in the house," Dad said at the same time that Theo said, "You always want to go out to dinner!" This was true. Aside from Beef Stroganoff, neither Dad nor I could really cook.

"Well, maybe I don't feel well tonight, or maybe I have other plans."

"You don't feel well?" my dad asked. "What's the matter?"

"I feel fine," I said. "But what if I didn't?"

"So what plans do you have?" Theo asked. "You didn't say any—"

"I didn't say I had something else to do. I just asked, what if I did? What if I was doing something with Julia?" I stopped. I didn't want to fight with him.

My dad looked amused; Theo looked baffled.

"Oh, whatever." I gave up. "Sure. Give me ten minutes to shower. Where do you want to go?"

Where Theo wanted to go was Manuelito's, a Mexican place near our school. He made a point of asking me if that was okay and I said it was.

As I headed into the house, my dad said to Theo, "Women," and Theo laughed. I knew my dad was teasing me, but it was still irritating.

Theo was watching the news with my dad when I came back. He stood up. "Don't worry, sir," he told my dad. "I'll get her back early."

"Have fun." My dad got up too and disappeared into the back of the house. The light in the kitchen went on, and I briefly wondered what he'd find to eat. Maybe I'd bring him back a taco.

Manuelito's was packed, and at first I didn't think we'd find a place to sit. Then Julia waved at me from a booth in the back. Her boyfriend, Justin, sat across from her. I nudged Theo and pointed.

"Oh, there they are!" he said.

"You knew they'd be here?"

He steered me past the game room and through the close-packed tables. "When you told me you were on your way home, I asked Justin to save us some seats. I figured you'd be craving flautas."

"Yay, rain!" Julia said as I slid into the booth next to her. Theo sat down across from me. "Yay, wind!" She put her arm around my shoulders and squeezed. She was so much shorter than me that she had to reach up, and her soft hair tickled my nose. "We can actually hang out together for more than five minutes, and on a Saturday!"

"There's nothing special about Saturdays for me," Theo pointed out. "I still have to go to work tomorrow."

"But not until the afternoon," Justin said. "I have to get up almost as early as Clancy." Justin had worked for his father's landscaping company every summer since he was a little kid and weekends were busy for them, but the pool where Theo worked didn't open until lunchtime on Sunday.

"If the weather gets better, I'm going rock climbing in the morning," Theo said. "Have to get in shape for the summer. The club has planned some really good trips to the mountains." He flexed his arms as though already imagining scaling a cliff, and the muscles on his upper arms rippled.

"Did you hear about that job at the miniature golf place?" I asked Julia.

"Yup, they want me to come back part-time and work with the little kids." Julia was crazy about kids, and they were crazy about her. She volunteered at a day care for under-privileged kids during the school year, and I had helped her put on a play with them over the winter.

"So, mostly weekends?" She nodded and we high-fived. I worked mostly on weekends too, and this meant we'd have time to get together during the week.

"I can do my homework at the DZ," I said. "The class I'm taking is self-paced—"

Justin interrupted me. "You're going to summer school? What, a 4.0 isn't enough for you?" He always tried to make me feel bad for doing well in school, like I was some kind of pathetic geek. I guess he was kidding, like Julia always said, but I didn't find it amusing, and sometimes I just wanted him to talk normally instead of always trying to be funny. I didn't say so because it would surely lead to, "Oh, poor Clancy, did I hurt your widdle feelings?"

I explained, trying to keep a patient kindergarten-teacher tone out of my voice, "It's just an online class. AP Art History. If I get the AP credit, I'll be able to start off with upper-level art history courses in college. I want to graduate in three years, and that'll be hard with a double major, so I'll need all the APs I can get."

Theo leaned across the table. "My nerdy girlfriend." He kissed me on the cheek. "I saw your light reading for the DZ that you left in the car. Come on, *National Geographic*?"

"I like that stuff about the Incas and the Aztecs. It's interesting, and it's something I should know about if I'm going to be an archaeologist."

"Missouri Jones doesn't have the same ring to it as Indiana Jones, though," Julia chimed in.

"Which were the ones that did human sacrifices—the Aztecs or the Incas?" Justin asked.

"Both." I waited, knowing that he'd follow this up with something that he thought was funny but I probably wouldn't.

Sure enough, he held his menu up to his face and peeked over its top at the waiter making the rounds. "Do you think he's Aztec or Inca? Better be careful what you order. You don't know where those sacrificed humans wind up."

"Justin!" Julia glared at him. "That's so racist!"

"Oh, come on," Justin said. "No way he could hear."

"Well, I heard you," Julia snapped. Justin was so clueless.

Julia's mom is Dominican, not Mexican, but still, what a jerk.

He managed to get her to forgive him by the time the waiter brought us all large Cokes and we ordered our usuals. Julia poked me in the ribs, and I looked down to see that she was holding out a small bottle of amber liquid to me under the table—rum, I guessed. She nodded at my Coke. Obviously, she meant for me to pour some of the rum into it. I shook my head.

"Oh, come on," she said. "Live a little. Celebrate the beginning of summer break. You're almost a junior."

"You know how my dad is," I said. "He always pretends he's just kissing me good night when really, he's smelling my breath for alcohol." She grimaced sympathetically and started to pass the bottle to Theo, but on an impulse I grabbed it from her, surprising myself as much as Julia. *What has gotten into me today?* Maybe I was tired of being predictable.

"Changed my mind," I whispered as I poured no more than a tablespoon of rum into my glass. *I'm not driving*, I reminded myself. *It's okay.*

"Well, will you look at that," Julia said.

Justin glanced down. He whistled under his breath. "Clancy Edwards, you are finally growing up."

I didn't answer as I handed Theo the bottle under the table. "What are you doing?" he asked in a low voice, giving the bottle back to Justin without taking any. He was Mr. Designated Driver. "Won't your dad—"

I was already regretting what I had done but tried to shrug it off. "I fear not the wrath of my sire." I waved a chip grandiosely in the air. "I'll just be sure to eat enough guacamole so my garlic breath covers it up."

The Coke barely tasted different, especially after the splash of rum was diluted with a refill, and the food was good, as always. Julia was even chattier than usual, which was also good, because I didn't feel like talking. That's what usually happened. When Julia and I were ten and first saw a yin-yang symbol, with the black shape and the white shape curling around each other and fitting together perfectly, we knew that was us. We were total opposites in most ways, but we fit together. She shook me out of my routine, and I reined in her craziness. It seemed that whenever she didn't want to talk, I did, and the other way around. Her mom always said that Julia would never open a book if it wasn't for me studying so much, and my dad liked how Julia would drag me out to movies and things when I'd been alone in my room for too long. We still drew the yin-yang symbol on each other's notebooks in school.

The guys didn't seem to notice how quiet I was, and as soon as they had wolfed down their enchiladas and chiles rellenos, they got up to play pinball.

Julia sucked the last of her Coke out of the glass. "So what's the matter?" she asked.

I shrugged and looked across the room to where Justin and Theo were battling it out. "Just tired, I guess." I didn't want to tell her that Theo was getting on my nerves, not after I had been obsessed with him since the first day of tenth grade, when he was newly arrived from Alabama. I got so excited when he finally asked me out in January that

I nearly fainted. Half the girls in our class had a crush on him, yet he chose me. I still couldn't believe it sometimes. Julia would think I was crazy if I suddenly said that Theo's never-ending attention was getting old. For her, the more attention, the better. Besides, it was probably just that I'd been in a weird mood ever since I'd been at the DZ. Ever since I'd met Denny.

"Maybe you can stay home tomorrow," Julia suggested. "Tell your dad you're sick."

I sighed and twisted my paper napkin around and around. "No, I need the money. The weather's supposed to be better tomorrow, and there'll be lots of students. Besides, if I don't go, my dad'll stay home, and then I'll feel guilty. And I can't go to Angie's, so my dad would have to find someone to stay with me." Angie had left for New Mexico in a hurry a few weeks earlier, when her son-in-law had walked out on her daughter, Leanne—my former babysitter—and their twins. Angie was going to take care of the grandkids until her son-in-law either came back or paid enough child support to pay for day care. Angie's son, Jackson, had just come home after finishing his freshman year of college and was watching the house.

"This is getting ridiculous," Julia said. "You're sixteen. You don't need a babysitter."

"Ha! It's not a babysitter he thinks I need. He doesn't think I need someone to make me dinner and keep me from falling down the stairs. It's a chaperone he wants."

"But Theo's working all day!"

"He's not worried about the daytime—it's after Theo

gets off work." I twirled the paper wrapper from my straw and sighed. "My dad must have been really wild and crazy when he was our age, because he keeps saying, 'I know what teenagers are like.'" I made my voice dark and growly, and Julia laughed. "He says that without a mother's influence, I need more supervision than other girls my age."

Julia was still laughing. "*You* need supervision? You need less supervision than anyone I know! You've never even broken curfew."

"Yes, I have—" I protested, but she wagged a finger at me.

"Five minutes late on Halloween when you're in high school doesn't count. You have the cutest boyfriend at Hawkins High and you're still a virgin. You don't drink, even though you could totally get away with it. You don't smoke, you're a straight-A student, you leave the room when someone even lights up a joint—"

"Secondhand smoke. My dad could whip out a drug-testing kit any minute."

"Oh, you know he'd never do that!"

I took a sip of Coke to untie the sudden knot in my throat. When I could speak, I said, "Jules, I can't do any-thing risky. You know that. It would kill him if something happened to me. It took him forever to get over my mom. I mean, he still hasn't gotten over her—he never talks about her or anything—but it took him forever to stop being a zombie."

"I know," she said. "But your dad's a big boy. You don't need to take care of him." It was an old argument, and I knew she didn't expect me to answer. She knew what I'd say anyway—that both of her parents were alive, even if they were divorced, and that although her dad lived in Vermont and she hardly ever saw him, it was totally different. She couldn't understand what it was like to have her mom die. She didn't know what it was like to see her dad with a wound that everyone thought was scarred over but that sometimes opened. I'd do anything to keep from reopening it myself.

"Anyway," she went on, "maybe he'll marry one of those women he keeps going out with, and he'll lighten up on you some."

"Maybe." I didn't feel hopeful.

We sat without speaking again, her head on my shoulder and my cheek on her hair, until the guys came back.

Justin looked us up and down. "Everything okay?"

"Just girl talk." Julia straightened up. "Where do you guys want to go now?" She squeezed my hand and released it.

"I got up at five o'clock this morning," I said, "and I have to get up at five tomorrow morning. I'm too tired to be any fun. I just want to go home and watch something stupid on TV and go to bed. You guys go on without me. Theo can take me home, and then go do whatever you two wind up doing."

Julia protested, but I could see that Justin thought it was a great idea. I gave Jules a hug and said good-bye to Justin, and Theo and I walked back to his car, our fingers entwined.

"So why the booze?" he asked.

"I don't know. Just wanted to see what the big deal was, I guess." But what I had really wanted was to see what it felt like to not always be a good girl, to do something that would upset my dad if he knew about it. I just had to make sure he never did know about it.

Even though it was June, the air was cool after the rain, and Theo's hand felt nice and warm. I matched my stride to his, and he kissed the top of my head and then my cheek. We stopped walking, and I turned to him. He held my face in both his hands and kissed me, gently and sweetly at first, and then, as I pressed myself into him, harder and more eagerly. His hand moved to my back and slid up under my T-shirt.

"Get a room!" Justin called from his car window as he and Julia took off, and Theo jumped back as though someone had hit him.

"Justin can be such a jerk." He sounded embarrassed.

"You speak sooth," I said. "He's a rank and arrant knave."

He chuckled and put his arm around me. "Well, I don't know that he's *that* bad. Jerk, maybe sometimes. 'Rank and arrant,' whatever that means—I don't know."

I rolled my eyes in theatrical disagreement, which made Theo laugh again.

"Come on," he said. "I'll take you home."

4

FACT: Since the 1970s, skydiving has recorded fewer casualties every decade, even though the number of people participating in the sport and the number of jumps have increased every decade.

—*The Whuffo's Guide to Skydiving*

My dad was dozing in his recliner with the TV on. I stood for a minute and watched him. He must have been exhausted. I wished he'd just go to bed when I was late coming home. My dad always said he wasn't waiting up for me, but that he got interested in a movie or couldn't sleep or got up to make a snack, but I noticed he never fell asleep in the recliner when I stayed home.

I switched the TV off. "Dad," I said. He grunted. "Dad, I'm home. Going to bed now." I started to go past him to get to my room, but he woke up enough to say, "Give your old dad a good-night kiss." I bent over to kiss his cheek, holding my breath.

"Garlic much?" He waved a hand in front of his face. He didn't say anything about me coming back early. He probably figured that Theo was being thoughtful by bringing me home before curfew, knowing that I had to get up early. I'd once heard him tell one of the Stroganoff ladies, "Theo takes such good care of her," like I was a puppy.

The next morning Dad had to call me three times before I dragged myself out of bed. The sun wasn't up yet, so the grass was damp and a bit of a chill still hung in the air. I lay down on the backseat as soon as I got in the car and wrapped myself in the afghan I kept in the car after fastening the seat belt, which I knew Dad would check. I pretended to fall asleep so I wouldn't have to talk if he got chatty. Pretty soon I did doze off, and I woke up only when we arrived at Skydive Knoxton.

I sat up and rubbed my eyes. The sky was turning from dawn orange to summer blue, and everything sparkled after the rain. I glanced at my reflection in the side mirror of the car. My eyes were red and puffy, and I was wearing the same T-shirt I had slept in. My hair is so thick that it had still been damp from my shower when I went to bed the night before, and now it poked out in all directions. When I ran my tongue over my teeth, I could tell that my hasty toothbrushing that morning had already worn off. No makeup, of course. The students would be so nervous and the regular jumpers would be so focused on what they were doing that no one would have noticed if I'd walked naked through the hangar. And there was no point in making the effort anyway, I had told myself, since I'd be folding canopies, stowing lines, and closing containers all day. The work was dusty, and even though it was only June, the metal roof of the hangar would turn the place into an oven by noon.

Why did I even look in the mirror then? *Denny might come back today*, something in me said.

"So what?" I said out loud, but I couldn't squelch the hope that he'd be there.

I hauled myself out of the car and picked up my book, even though with the beautiful weather, we'd probably have so many students that I'd be too busy to read. Mentally, I added up how much money I was likely to earn. If I thought about the weather and money, I wouldn't think about Denny. The only reason I was thinking about him at all was because he was fun to talk to, I told myself.

In the office, Cynthia was passing out forms to four students, three guys and a girl. No Denny. The realization brought a sour feeling of disappointment, followed immediately by guilt that I was disappointed. *You're overreacting, Carys Clancy*, I told myself firmly. No more late nights before work—I got emotional too easily when I didn't sleep enough. That explained my mood.

Today wouldn't be nearly as interesting. The first jumpers looked like they'd been up all night partying. They had probably gone out to fortify themselves the night before and had gotten so wired they couldn't sleep. Cynthia rattled off what they had to sign and what pages they had to initial, and the four of them settled down with papers and clipboards. There was the usual nervous joking, and when my dad came in they stood up and crowded around him. That's the way it always was. Cynthia is cute and little, with strawberry blonde hair and big green eyes, and although lots of male students and some female ones flirt with her, they always seem to think she won't give them the right information. *Just let them see her skydive*, I thought, picturing how ferociously she swoops into a landing, always standing it up. She looks like an angel with her powder-blue canopy settling behind her. But my dad is big, and more importantly, he's male, so jump students always act like cubs pawing at the big-maned lion for attention and reassurance.

"Much safer than hang gliding," he said in answer to a question I hadn't heard. "Safer than downhill skiing. Think about it. When you're jumping there are only two variables: the person jumping and the equipment. I only hire instructors who've made at least twenty tandem jumps. And our equipment exceeds all of USPA's requirements."

"USPA?" asked a skinny guy wearing a Clemens T-shirt.

"United States Parachute Association," Dad said. "Anyway, compare skydiving to downhill skiing. When you're skiing you have those same two variables: the person and the equipment, just like in jumping. But there are other things that can go wrong on the ski slopes. You're surrounded by skiers who might not know what they're doing, but when you're doing a jump you know that the other jumpers around you are experts. Plus, there are trees and cliffs and slick spots on a ski slope. None of that in the sky."

He laid a hand on the guy's shoulder and looked into his eyes. I knew that look. It was tough and warm at the same time, unlike the way he looked at me, like he was sure I was about to break. He trusted a stranger, someone he'd never seen before, someone whose name he didn't even know, to make a good jump, but not me.

As though echoing my thought, my dad said to the guy, "Trust me. You'll have the time of your life."

And, as always, the student looked about six shades less pale and even stood up a little straighter. He picked up his pen and initialed all the paragraphs that said he understood the risk of injury or fatality, and that he wouldn't sue anybody if he wound up paralyzed or dead.

I loaded my coffee with extra milk powder and sugar since it would have to be my breakfast until I took a mid-morning break at the café next to the airport. I waved at Leon and Noel, who were just coming in, and squeezed past the students and out the door to the hangar. I didn't have anything to pack yet, so I settled on my beanbag chair and opened my textbook. I always felt more comfortable if I already knew the basics of the topic before classes started.

For some reason the art of the Cycladic islands wasn't as appealing as I had thought it would be. My mind wandered away from a theory of what the Cycladic people's religion might have been like, and when someone paused in the doorway of the hangar, casting a long shadow across the floor, I felt my heart lift a little with the hope that it was Denny.

It wasn't; just someone looking for my dad.

There was no reason for him to be there, I told myself as I tried to concentrate on my reading. Skydive Knoxton had a higher rate of repeat business than most DZs, but it was still only around ten percent, compared with the average of five percent, and college students were rarely among the few who came back.

And why should I care one way or the other?

So it was almost spooky when I was leafing through an ancient book of my dad's called *United We Fall*, and a quiet voice behind me said, "Hey."

I nearly dropped the book. Of course it was Denny. "What are you doing here?" I asked before I could stop myself from sounding rude.

"Came back for another jump." He looked as awkward as I felt.

"Cynthia's checking in a bunch of first-timers," I said. "You'll probably be on the load after them."

"Thanks. I'll sign up when she's done. What are you reading?"

I looked down. "This?" I stuck some pages back in the book after they fluttered to the floor. "It's about formation skydiving. Or RW. Relative work. You know, when jumpers in freefall make formations with each other."

"I meant that one actually." He pointed to the art history book.

"Oh, this is for a class I'm taking this summer. It's a prerequisite for some upper-level classes."

"What's your major?"

I answered, "I'm planning to double in anthro and art

history," and then I realized he must think I was a college student.

"I'm starting at Clemens next fall," he said before I could correct his wrong impression. "I just got here. I'm doing an internship in Springfield this summer."

So that was why he'd been texting so much yesterday: a summer apart from a girlfriend back home. "What in?" I asked.

"Psychology. Mostly I'll be cleaning out monkey cages. Do you have any idea how bad monkey poop smells?" I shook my head. "Well, I won't go into it, but I'm not thrilled about smelling it all summer."

"Do they do anything mean to the monkeys?"

"Hope not. I don't really know yet. I just got here on Friday, and they gave me a tour and said to come back on Monday."

"Are you living on campus?"

"No, in an apartment. It's right near the college, though. I can walk to the lab."

"Are you pre-med?"

"I'm thinking psych. What about you? Why the double major?"

"It's for archaeology. I should probably minor in something like history or geology."

"Cool. Archaeology would be amazing. Don't you have to go to school for like years before you can do it?"

"Probably no longer than for becoming a psychologist," I pointed out.

"I'm not for sure going to be a psychologist. That's why

I'm doing the internship, to see if I like it. So have you gone on any digs or anything?"

"No." I stopped before telling him I was probably too young. It wasn't any of his business how old I was.

"I bet there's a dig around here someplace," he said. "Maybe they have internships too. You could find out whether you like being in the bottom of a trench in the middle of the summer." That had always been the only unappealing part of archaeology to me. I figured there had to be digs in places that didn't get as hot as Missouri. It was a school field trip to ruins of ancient Native American mounds in Charleston, Missouri, that had gotten me thinking about archaeology in the first place.

"It would probably be really hot," I admitted. "But just think of all the amazing things left to discover. I was thinking of underwater archaeology, actually."

"Cool," Denny said again. "You scuba dive?"

Again I had to say no. I felt like a little kid who said I wanted to be an astronaut when I grew up without having any idea what astronauts did, like you could show up at NASA one day and get put into a rocket ship. Before I could change the subject, he asked me another question.

"And don't archaeologists usually find just little pieces of pots and things anyway, not marble statues and gold jewelry and whole temples like in *National Geographic*?"

I couldn't help sounding exasperated that he was shooting down my Indiana Jones fantasies. "Okay, so maybe they do, but somebody has to find the statues and temples and jewelry. Why not me?"

"Why not you?" he agreed, and he smiled. He had a great smile that crinkled up the skin around his eyes. It almost made me stop being annoyed at the way he was interrogating me. Everyone else said that archaeology was great and I'd be a terrific archaeologist. Nobody asked about the details like this, and it made me uncomfortable to be questioned so closely by a stranger.

Do I wish now, knowing everything that happened next, that I'd told him I was in high school and was only sixteen? Everything would have been different. Most people would say that everything would have been better.

And maybe it would here. But even so, if I had it all to do over again, I know I'd let him go on thinking I was a college student and eighteen years old. Because even with what happened, there's nothing that I would trade for that summer.

Accelerated Free Fall (AFF): One or two skydiving instructors exit the aircraft with the student, help her remain stable, and move away only when she has demonstrated awareness and the ability to deploy the parachute.

—*The Whuffo's Guide to Skydiving*

5

"So what made you decide to make a jump this summer?" I asked Denny, to change the subject. Plus, I was being friendly to a client. My dad would approve.

His smile disappeared. Odd—usually first jumpers are thrilled to talk about what inspired them to skydive. "It's just . . . it's something I've wanted to do for a long time. I was only going to do the one jump yesterday, but then I changed my mind. I'm going again." He looked out at the landing area. "This time I want to do it without someone else doing all the work."

"You're doing an AFF?" This doesn't happen often. It's more expensive than a tandem jump since there's a half day of class and practice, and then the jumper has to pay for two instructors, not just one. Most AFF students are interested in more than the adrenaline rush and want to learn the sport side of it. Others want to prove something to themselves. I wondered which kind Denny was. Either way, I respected AFF students more than tandems. If you're just going for an adrenaline rush, why not do a bungee jump instead of a skydive? It's cheaper and quicker.

Over the PA, Cynthia said, "Load one to the hangar," and the first group of jump students came in through the wide door, chatting nervously. Randy—my least favorite instructor—and Noel followed them, and Randy beckoned me over to where the student rigs were laid out on the floor.

"'Scuse me," I said to Denny.

"Rig this one up, would you?" Randy pointed at one of the guys in the group. I recognized him from the week before, when Patsy had been training him in AFF. Randy consulted the sheet of paper in his hand. "His name's Travis. He's the only one not doing a tandem. Patsy's running late but she should be here in time to take him out with Mad Jack. I'll brief the tandem students while you're doing that." He winked. "And I'll owe you one."

I ignored the wink and introduced myself to Travis. I told him to step into the leg straps and pull them up over his knees. "Now put on the harness like you're putting on a jacket," I said. He pulled the straps over his shoulders. I tightened the leg straps around his thighs, then the chest band and the belly band. I tucked the ends of the straps into their keepers. "Can you breathe okay?"

Travis nodded. He was pale. "You're not the one I'm going to jump with, are you?" His voice shook a little and he cleared his throat.

"No, I'm just helping. Patsy and Jack are taking you out. Don't worry—they'll be here any minute and they'll check everything before you get in the plane, and then they'll check it again before you go out the door. And someone will check their gear too." I'd said those words so many times that my voice sounded mechanical to me. Maybe it did to Travis too; he didn't look any calmer.

The group of tandem students laughed at something Randy said. I wished I could make Travis laugh to relax him some, but he was too tightly wound up. He wiped a trail of sweat off his forehead. It was warm in the hangar, but not *that* warm. This was obviously fear-sweat.

Randy was flirting like crazy with one of the girls, and I could tell he had staked her out to jump with. Since the girl was pretty, he'd probably hit on her. In the adrenaline rush and the high of landing safely, she might say yes when she would otherwise say no. Randy's pretty hot—slender and wiry, with thick brown hair and a square jaw—but it's really his confidence that makes him so attractive. The difference between Randy and other alpha males, like my dad and Theo, is that they used their powers for good, not evil.

I tugged everything to ensure it was snug. "All set. Have fun." *Be sure to remind them it's fun*, my dad always said. *That's something students tend to forget when it comes right down to it*. But if you have to remind them it's fun, how much fun is it, exactly? Or is it only fun once the scary part is over? Everyone says that on your first jump, the second you feel opening shock and the canopy looks good overhead, you feel so safe that you can finally relax and enjoy it.

Travis must have been one of the people who forget that it's fun, because he grabbed my hand. His fingers were icy and clammy. "What if I change my mind once I'm up there?" he asked in a hoarse whisper. "Would they push me out?"

"No, they can't do that. No one can make you jump—not your instructor, not your girlfriend"—I glanced at the girl Randy was flirting with—"not anybody. You shouldn't let anyone pressure you into it. You just have to say that you changed your mind. Patsy won't care. Just make sure you tell her before you're in the door of the plane. She might not be able to hear you, and it might be hard to get back in once you're at the edge."

I shouldn't have said that last part; he turned greenish. "You've done it lots of times, right?" he asked. "How long before you stop being scared?"

"Don't worry!" I sounded fake to myself, but he looked like he was grabbing a lifeline I had thrown him. "You'll be fine once you're out there."

He still looked doubtful, but then Patsy rushed in and spared me having to go on by saying, "Sorry, sorry—I got stuck in traffic. How you feeling?"

Patsy has a magical way of making people comfortable,

and Travis instantly looked better. While she was giving him last-minute instructions, I headed back to the packing table. Denny was gone; he must have headed inside to the office, becoming one of the ten percent who cash in their discount certificate.

My dad poked his head out of the classroom in the back of the hangar. "C.C., could you come here?" I went in and looked around. My dad mustn't have been inside the classroom for weeks—he didn't teach much AFF—and there were piles of things all over, and dust. "Clear this stuff out," he said.

"To hear is to obey, my liege!"

He made an impatient face, but he knew how much I hated it when he barked orders at me. "Please."

"Shouldn't I be packing?"

"That can wait. We have another AFF student, and this place is a mess."

I rolled the wheelbarrow in. I'd been itching to clean up the classroom anyway. Disorder makes me crazy. I scooped everything off the table and into the wheelbarrow while my dad tossed in things from the floor: old jumpsuits, papers, a cracked helmet—a sight not likely to add to a student's confidence, even though it had been run over, not damaged in a jump accident—and other junk.

The wheelbarrow screeched as I rolled it away. I did a few more loads and then left it in the corner like my dad had said. There was a lull now and then, but I was too restless to read my textbook. I checked my phone, but there was nothing from Theo.

I should have been pleased that he was giving me some space, but it felt weird that he wasn't checking on me.

Putting things in order was soothing, and besides, I could look on the trash as an archaeological project. I unearthed lots of back issues of *Jump!* magazine, none of them old enough to be historical, just enough to be uninteresting. They had articles about new gear; photos of people getting awards for reaching a thousand jumps; and lists of records, like the most women over forty in one formation, and the largest number of amputees in a single formation.

I tossed the cracked helmet into a big trash can, along with some pieces of ripstop nylon and three right-handed jump gloves with no corresponding left. I didn't think we'd need them; we weren't planning an amputee record attempt anytime soon. Next was a mouse's nest—empty but smelly—which I held out to Ripstop, who had just strolled over. "Isn't that what you're here for? Killing mousies?" I tossed it out.

I picked up a logbook, one of the standard black spiral-bound notebooks with places to record jump altitude and maneuvers and things like that, just like the ones that my dad had used when he started sport jumping after he got back from Iraq. He still sold them from the office. This one belonged to an AFF student, Margaret Finnegan. I vaguely remembered her—she had a skydiving boyfriend who talked her into doing AFF. According to the logbook, she had done the whole sequence. Then nothing. I vaguely remembered that she'd sprained her ankle or something on her solo.

That was about a year ago, but Cynthia probably still had her address, so I stuck the logbook on the shelf I used for my personal stuff, including the box where I kept my tips. My dad's name was still on my bank account, and I didn't want him to know how much I had saved up. My plans to go away to college were a touchy subject. I'd use my own money to apply to colleges out of state and wouldn't mention it to him. If I got into a good school with a good archaeology program, and if I'd saved up enough *and* got a scholarship, that's when we'd have it out. As soon as I turned eighteen, I would open up my own account.

That shelf also held the notebook of skydiving facts and definitions that I had started in middle school after I shocked a teacher with a casual reference to a horny gorilla. She called my dad, who laughed for so long that he could hardly convince her that it was the name of a skydiving maneuver. I started the notebook after that, in self-defense. I called it "The Whuffo's Guide to Skydiving," and I tried to make it sound like a serious reference work. It sat on the shelf with Dad's old skydiving books, some ancient *National Geographic*s, my art history text, and now Margaret Finnegan's logbook.

The jumpers from the first load came back in. Randy was still working his magic on his tandem student. Travis looked gloomy as the girl laughed and posed for the camera with her arm around Randy's waist, his around her shoulders. Then Travis and Patsy and Mad Jack, who was his other instructor, went out with some fun jumpers to get on the next load.

I stretched out the lines of Randy's rig and made everything smooth. I flaked the canopy and pulled the slider into place, then stowed the lines and closed the pack. When I reached for the other rig, I saw Denny come in from the direction of the office. He was with my dad and Louisa.

I've known Louisa forever. She was one of the Sky-Witches—my mom's demo team, the one that jumped into football games and concerts and things like that—and she was on my mom's last load. She'd been under canopy when my mom had her accident, so she saw it all from the air. My dad saw it too, but from the ground. Not me. I was asleep in the lounge behind the office, coming down with the flu, although nobody knew that at the time.

Louisa gave me a wink before the three of them went into the classroom at the back of the hangar, and I started on another rig.

My phone pinged and I leaped for it. It wasn't Theo; just Julia, who wanted to know if I could go with her to get a summer haircut on Monday. I told her I'd ask.

Business was slower than it had been on Saturday morning—people were probably in church hoping they'd get holy enough to go to heaven if they died during their jump—and my dad had gone out with Norton and Mad Jack. Dad was always in a good mood after a jump since he hardly ever had the time to jump for fun anymore, so it was the best time to ask him. I found him in the office, where he was doing some bookkeeping.

He looked up over his glasses. "Hey, C.C. What's up?"

"Julia wants me to go with her to get a haircut tomorrow.

She asked if she could pick me up." I could see refusal starting to form in his mind, so I went on hurriedly, "She's had her license for nine months, and the salon is so close. She won't have to go on any busy streets." It didn't look like he was weakening. "Come on, I don't want my daddy to take me everyplace like it's the first day of kindergarten." Only he hadn't been the one to take me that day. My mom had, and all summer she'd made school sound like so much fun that I was so excited that I hardly even noticed when she left me.

"Sorry, hon." He shook his head. "I like Julia, I really do, but I don't trust her driving. I saw that dent in her fender when she came by the other day. How did that happen?"

"I don't know." I did know; it was just a fender bender, and the way Julia told it, it was kind of the other guy's fault too. But my dad would never believe that.

"And I've seen her texting at the wheel, and—"

"All *right*!" I spat. "I get it. I can't ride with her. Fine. You can be my taxi service until I go to . . ." I stopped. If I had said "until I go to college," he would have jumped on that and said he could still drive me then—Clemens wasn't too far away.

I stomped out before I completely lost it. I was seething, clenching my teeth so I wouldn't shout at him. He was being utterly and completely ridiculous. So Julia texted while she was driving. . . . She knew I didn't like it and didn't do it when I was in the car unless we were at a red light. And anyone can have a fender bender.

I texted Julia and said I'd come but I'd have to take a bus.

Then I flung a rig on the table and slammed it together. I tossed it on the "done" pile and grabbed another one. After the third, the repetitive motions did their work and calmed me down enough so that I could breathe normally.

I texted Theo to ask when he was getting off work. He answered that he had to stay late and help with pool maintenance, so seeing each other that evening was out, but that he'd pick me up the next day and we'd go to lunch, just the two of us, no Julia or Justin. I squelched my irritation that he didn't ask me first, assuming that of course I'd be okay with his plans, and I answered that he could pick me up at Julia's salon at eleven o'clock.

"Argh!" I shouted, tossing my phone on the table. Would anybody ever allow me to make up my mind for myself? I looked around. No one seemed to have heard me, and if they had, they'd probably think I was having a hard time untangling lines or something.

I heard yelling from the classroom. I needed a break, so I went over and peeked in to see what was going on. Denny dangled in a harness a few feet off the ground, looking extremely foolish, while Louisa tried to fluster him. Neither one of them appeared to notice me.

"You have line twists!" Louisa shouted. "They're holding your canopy closed, and you're falling too fast!" She grabbed him by the leg and gave a mighty heave, and he twirled in the air, hanging from the pretend parachute. "Do something!" She kept yelling while he yanked at the lines and looked at her hopefully.

She sighed. "Dude. I'm not up there with you. There's

no one up there with you. You're in the freaking *air*, and you're all *alone*, and you're coming down too fast. You're going to make a bi-i-i-ig crater when you hit the ground."

Whomp! I said to myself. I swallowed.

"So what do you do?" She twirled him around again.

"I don't know." He sounded sheepish.

She sighed. "Well, you're dead now, so let's run through it once more and then you can try again. You don't just pull the lines once. If you don't clear the twist, you pull them again, and then you check your altimeter. Got it?"

He nodded.

"All right then. Okay, you just opened. What do you do?"

He looked up.

"Right, check the canopy. It looks all weird and bunched up because the lines got tangled when it tried to open. You start spinning and you're coming down too fast." She twirled him around and he yanked the lines.

"No good. Still tangled." Louisa increased the spin.

He yanked again, and again. "Did it clear?"

"Nope."

"So what do I do if pulling on the lines doesn't clear it?" He sounded frustrated.

"Look at your altimeter." Denny waited for more instruction. "Go ahead, look at it!" He raised his wrist to his face like he was reading a watch. "It says you're at three thousand feet. What do you do?"

"Um . . ."

"Clock's ticking. You're dropping. You have about thirty seconds of life left. Do you want 'um' to be your last word?"

"But won't the reserve open automatically?"

"Dude." She sighed again. "Look up. Your main is partially open. That'll probably slow you down so much that the reserve won't be triggered. And if it did, what if the two canopies got tangled with each other?"

I felt sick.

"Oh right!" Denny's face brightened. He let go of the steering toggles and fumbled with the cutaway handle on his right shoulder.

"Say it out loud!" Louisa barked.

"Look red," Denny said as he looked down at the red plastic handle. "Hands red." He grabbed the handle with both hands and hesitated.

"You're falling!" Louisa said. "No good canopy!"

"Look silver." Denny turned his head to look at the reserve deployment handle on his left shoulder. "Pull red. Pull silver." He yanked the red handle to jettison his main canopy, and then the silver one to open the reserve.

"Congratulations," Louisa said. "You just saved your own life. Remember, the AAD—"

"The what?" he interrupted.

"Automatic Activation Device. It fires the reserve automatically if you're going too fast below a preset altitude. Reserves hardly ever malfunction, but don't count on that. Open it yourself as soon as you've cut away the main. Remember this about your reserve: *when in doubt, whip it out.*"

Denny said, almost fiercely, "Do it again."

Louisa set him spinning so fast his head wobbled. He pulled on the lines three times, looked at the dummy altimeter on his wrist, pulled on the cutaway handle, and then made the motions of dumping the reserve. He swung around and then back again slowly as the momentum of Louisa's shove wore off.

"You're alive!" Louisa gave him a big smile. She pushed him backward until his feet were above the table and lowered him gently. I wondered if his legs had gone to sleep from dangling for so long.

I pulled back quickly before they could see me. I knew they'd practice it again and again until Louisa was sure that if Denny got line twists under canopy, he wouldn't have to think about what to do, but would just react. She'd make him practice clearing bag locks and partial deployments and even extremely rare things like getting the pilot chute wrapped around his leg—nothing to do for that but cut the line with his hook knife and open the reserve and pray for no entanglement. Finally, he'd learn how to head into the wind under canopy and how to land. It would take at least four hours, depending on how well he did. My dad had the most expensive AFF course in the state, but it was also the one with the fewest accidents.

Then Denny would jump and prove to himself or to whoever he kept texting or to his parents that he could do it, and he'd go to his internship on Monday and casually mention that he'd jumped out of a plane over the weekend, not just once but twice, and he would become the biggest deal in the lab for the day, and then he'd clean up monkey poop all summer.

And I would pack rigs every weekend and go out with

Theo and study art history and then go back to school for junior year, and everything would go along on its predictable path.

When I heard them finishing up in the classroom, I went into the office instead of the hangar so that Denny wouldn't think I was waiting for him, which was stupid—he knew I was there to work. Then I went outside to watch. I shaded my eyes and stared up at the plane, which turned in the sky to set up for jump run. It looked like they'd gone all the way to the full fourteen thousand feet.

A little cluster of tandem students stood at the fence saying, "No way I would go out the door by myself" and things like that. Patsy and Randy had come out to watch; an AFF student was enough of a novelty to pass the time between loads. Leon was out on the field, ready to talk Denny into his landing via the radio in his helmet. My dad and Louisa were of course in the plane, probably joking around to relax Denny, acting like falling almost three miles on purpose was just an ordinary thing people did every day. Which it was to them.

The engine noise dropped a little. "There's the cut," Randy said unnecessarily; Patsy and I had heard it too, and the students watching wouldn't know what it meant: that the pilot had cut the engine back a little so they'd be going slower when the jumpers exited.

First, the tandems came out, and then someone was standing in the door of the plane. Must be Mad Jack, who was shooting Denny's video. He dropped, and an instant later a knot of people fell through the door and smoothed into a three-way formation. It had to be my dad and Louisa with Denny in the middle. The tiny dot of Mad Jack fell with them, hanging just outside their formation. They were falling nice and stable.

Elsewhere in the sky, the tandem canopies opened—one, two, three, four—but I hardly paid attention. My dad and Louisa tracked away from Denny, and for an instant he was falling all alone. I'd heard that this was the scariest moment for a student. I wondered what he was feeling—exhilarated and powerful? Terrified? Confused? For a moment a longing to find out for myself filled my chest, but I squelched it.

Denny was close enough that I could see his arm move in toward his hip and then out again. He was too far away for me to see the pilot chute come out, but it must have, because suddenly the canopy unfurled like a huge green-and-white-striped flag and flew over his head.

"Good for him," Patsy said softly, and I wondered if she was remembering her own first AFF. I wondered what it felt like when opening shock jerked you so hard it could give you whiplash, but you didn't care because it meant that your canopy was open and you'd saved your own life. I wondered if the grab of the leg straps hurt or if you even felt it at all, and I imagined how beautiful even an ugly canopy must look because it was carrying you safely to the ground, and all you had left to do was steer yourself to the landing area, face into the wind, and touch the ground again.

I wondered if I'd ever know.

6

Flare: Right before touching down, the jumper flares (pulls down on both steering toggles at the same time). Flaring slows both the forward speed and the rate of descent, making for a safer and more comfortable landing.

—The Whuffo's Guide to Skydiving

Of course Denny tried to stand up his landing, but even though he faced into the wind and flared at just the right moment thanks to Leon's radioed instructions, he tumbled onto his face. He jumped up, though, and shouted, "Woo-hoo!" Louisa and my dad high-fived him, and Louisa hugged him.

I didn't want Denny to know I'd been watching, so I went back into the hangar and started packing again. Soon he came in, with his rig bundled up in his arms. "Where do you want this?" he asked. Despite a grin big enough to give him chipmunk cheeks, his face shone with tears.

"Over there." I gestured with my chin and turned back

to the packing table so he could wipe off his face without me looking at him. "So how was it?"

He dropped the rig on the floor. "Oh my God. Awesome. Amazing. The best thing I've ever done. I don't see why you're not up there all the time." I pretended I needed to concentrate on what I was doing.

He came closer. I could feel the excitement radiating off him and smell his adrenaline. "Can I help?"

I shook my head. "Only two people are supposed to pack a rig. A rigger"—I wasn't technically a rigger, but whatever—"or the person jumping the rig."

"So if I'm going to make another jump, I could pack that one?"

"Not unless you're going to do another tandem. This is a tandem rig." I stopped what I was doing and turned to face him. "*Are* you going to make another jump?"

He nodded. "But your dad wants me to wait a week. To give me a chance to process this one, he said."

Denny couldn't have been earning much, if anything, as an intern. His parents must have been paying for his jumps, although some parents freak out at the thought of their kid jumping out of a plane and refuse to pay for it. They had to have a lot of money—tandems are pretty expensive, and the AFF course costs over a thousand.

Not my business, though. I lifted another bundle of nylon and rope onto the table. This rig had gotten messed up, so I had to focus. Without raising my head, I asked Denny, "Aren't you going to call her and tell her about it?" I wished the words back in my mouth the instant I said them.

He asked, "Her? Who's her?"

"Whoever you were talking to yesterday after your tandem."

"Oh. That wasn't a her. That was a him."

"Sorry," I mumbled.

He didn't seem to hear me, and he swiped at his phone. Then he held it out to me. I squinted through the light filtering in the open door.

It was a picture of a boy about my age, with spiky black hair and startling blue eyes, wearing what looked like a track uniform and laughing at the camera. Very handsome. Denny swiped his thumb over the picture and the next one came up. I bit my lip. It was obviously the same guy, but this time his smile seemed forced, his hair was gone, and there were dark circles under his blue eyes, which looked faded somehow. His face was puffy, and he was leaning back in a recliner, looking like he could barely hold his head up.

Denny turned the phone toward himself and looked at it before sliding it back in his pocket. "My best friend. Not my boyfriend, if that's what you were thinking. His name's Frederick." His lips curled in a little smile. "If you call him Fred or Freddy he—well, let's say he doesn't react well. It's Frederick."

"Or F-bomb?"

"Did I say that? Yes, but I'm the only one who can call him that."

"What's the matter with him?" I hoped it was okay to ask, but I figured Denny wouldn't have shown me the second picture if he didn't expect me to be curious.

"Leukemia."

"Jeez." I didn't know much about leukemia, only that it was a kind of blood cancer and that people sometimes died from it. "How long's he had it?" I felt tentative asking about such a personal thing, but Denny didn't seem to mind.

"Since winter break, sophomore year. Or at least that's when they diagnosed it. He hadn't been feeling well for a few months, so he'd probably had it for a while by then."

"Is he going to be okay?"

Denny shrugged. His face was hard, as though he was trying not to show any expression. "Don't know. He felt great for a while after his first round of treatment. He came back to school and everything, but then he got sick again."

I didn't really know Denny at all, plus I'd never known anyone my age who was that sick. Would it be better to ask another question or change the subject? Say something optimistic or be sympathetic? I never knew how to talk about someone who had died or might be going to die, even though people seemed to think I should. What I did know was that when people say your life can change in an instant, that's only half the story. It's not just your life that changes. It's you. You become a whole different person. You go from being a girl whose parents jump out of airplanes to being a girl whose mother is dead, or from being a guy with a best friend to being a guy with a maybe-dying best friend. I knew without him telling me that people at school treated him differently than before, and that he even thought of himself differently.

I couldn't say any of this—I didn't want Denny to

think I was assuming Frederick would die. Denny seemed to want to talk about it, though. "They did chemo, which sucked, and then they tried some experimental thing with his immune system, but that made him even worse. So they did a bone-marrow transplant yesterday morning."

"Sounds serious."

"It's kind of the last thing they try. It makes you really sick, and a lot of people die from them, so they don't do it unless you're for sure going to die without it."

"So are you going home now to spend time with him?"

Denny gazed out the door at the bright sky, the colorful canopies, the happy people landing and laughing and whooping. "I wish. But Denver's too far. Anyway, I couldn't see him even if I was there. They killed his bone marrow to get rid of his immune system. Everything in his room has to be sterile, like in one of those bubbles, you know? He can't have a phone, and his own parents can't even touch him. They have to talk to him through a sheet of plastic. He'll be really sick for a long time before he gets better. *If* he gets better. He won't be able to see anyone else for weeks, not even his little brother."

He stopped and blushed. "Sorry. I don't know why I'm unloading on you like this. It's just—just so strange for me to be jumping out of a plane without him. We were supposed to do it together." He cleared his throat and looked away.

"It's okay." I felt like I should put my hand on his arm or even give him a hug. Julia would have done that, but I felt too awkward. "Is that why you did your jump yesterday— because they were doing the bone-marrow thing then?"

He nodded. "It seems pretty stupid, doesn't it? Like we're making a leap into an uncertain future together. He said I shouldn't shave my head when he lost his hair, and he told me to eat cheeseburgers and pizza in front of him, even when he was nauseous. He made me come here for the internship. But I had to do *something*. I couldn't just let him go through this alone. I felt like if I made a skydive and lived, then Frederick would live too. Like I said, pretty stupid."

I didn't think it was stupid at all, but I just said, "Hope he gets better."

Denny exhaled a big poof of air. "Thanks. It helps to talk about it. Everyone at home knows, so there's nothing to tell them. And I don't think it's what I should lead with on my first day at work tomorrow."

"I can see how that would be awkward. Leading with skydiving will make a *much* better first impression," I agreed, relieved that he didn't seem to feel weird for opening up to me.

Denny leaned on the table and watched me finish the rig.

"Hey, is there anywhere nearby to get lunch except that place next door?" he asked. "I ate there yesterday, and I can still taste it. Not a good taste either."

"My sympathies," I said. "I only go there for doughnuts, which they don't make. I haven't eaten anything they cook themselves since I was old enough to bring a PB&J from home."

"So is there anywhere else?"

"Sure, there are three diners in Knoxton. They're all on the main road."

He looked flustered. "I can draw you a map," I offered, but he said, "That's okay, I know how to get into town. I just wanted—unless you're really looking forward to your PB&J, do you want to have lunch with me? My treat. I owe you for saving my life. Twice."

Awkward. What now? I couldn't tell him that my daddy wouldn't let me go in his car without an interrogation. He must have noticed my hesitation because he said, "It's okay. I'm pretty gloomy these days, and I don't blame you for not wanting to hear more death and dying stories."

"No, that's not it," I said hastily. "It's just that my dad needs me here." I gestured at the rigs. "There are a lot of students today—"

"Sure, I understand," Denny said. "I should probably get back anyway. I'll see you next week if the weather cooperates." He turned to leave.

"Don't forget your video!" I called to him. "Maybe someone can show it to Frederick through the plastic thing."

"Oh thanks," he said. "Good idea. I totally forgot about it."

"Text me the link so I can see it too." I scribbled down my cell number.

He took the paper. "I'll only send it if I don't look like a total dork." He waved good-bye and headed toward the office.

I tugged on the nylon canopy on the table to straighten it out. My hair fell around my face, so I pulled an elastic out of my pocket and yanked it back into a ponytail. It was getting hot in the hangar, so I took off my long-sleeved shirt. I was already dreading July.

I went into the office for a bottle of water. Cynthia had finished logging in the paperwork of the last batch of students and was filing the forms they'd filled out. She looked up when I took a bottle of water out of the cooler. "Where's my dad?" I asked.

"Training another AFF student. One of the tandems got so hopped up when she saw Denny landing that she upgraded to AFF. Need something?"

"No, thanks." My dad would be busy for at least a few hours. I looked out the window and saw Denny walking to the parking lot, to have lunch all alone right after spilling his guts about Frederick. Maybe he was okay with that, but I didn't know him well enough to be sure. Then I remembered the tears on his cheeks, and on an impulse I asked, "Cyn, if I go to town for lunch, could you get someone to pack for me?"

She raised an eyebrow. Cynthia knew how much I needed money. But she just said, "Sure. It'll give Randy something to do other than hit on all the girl students."

"Thanks!" I said and ran out the door. I scanned the parking lot. A little sports car the color of a cherry Life Saver turned toward the exit. It slowed as the driver's window rolled down, and rock music blared. The driver turned down the volume, and Denny's head stuck out the window.

"Clancy?"

This was Denny's car? Well, I guess I didn't have to wonder whether his parents could afford the AFF course.

"Can I change my mind? About going to lunch, I mean?" I asked in a rush.

He grinned and leaned over to unlock the passenger-side door. As I got in I silently begged the gods of the drop zone that my dad would never, ever find out about this. Theo either.

Oops. What should I do about Theo? I could tell Denny that I had a boyfriend, but maybe he would think it was weird that I assumed he was interested in me as something other than a parachute packer. But if I didn't tell him, and he really was asking me out, I'd have to explain about Theo later, which would make me feel like I'd been leading him on.

I'd have to find some way to work Theo into the conversation.

"So where are we going?" Denny asked.

"We have three choices. We could go to a place with old-timey country food or a place with old-fashioned country food or a place with home-style country food. Take your pick."

He pretended to consider it seriously. "Oh, I think old-timey, if that's okay with you."

"That makes it Adrienne's." I directed him to Knoxton's one-block-long business street.

The familiar smell of coffee and fried food hit me when Denny opened the glass door. I directed him toward my favorite server's station, and before we even sat down, Melissa had set a Coke, no ice, on the table. "That's still your drink, I hope."

"Nectar of the gods." I took a sip. I left my phone on the table so I could see if my dad called me. I hoped he wouldn't notice I had left, but if by chance he called and I didn't answer, the next thing I knew he'd be phoning the police. If he didn't have a heart attack first.

"Chicken and dumplings today," Melissa told me. That had always been my favorite. She turned to Denny. "And for you?"

"I think I'd better have the chicken and dumplings too."

"Smart boy." Melissa looked at me approvingly. She leaned in and stage-whispered, "I'll just leave you two alone." I wanted to tell her that Denny wasn't my boyfriend, but it felt awkward, so I just smiled back, hoping he hadn't heard her. I also hoped she wouldn't say anything about high school in front of him.

Melissa brought two salads and two big steaming bowls full of chunks of chicken swimming in yellow gravy and puffy dumplings floating on top. Denny took a tentative bite, and then gave a little groan and rolled his eyes heavenward. The food kept the conversation limited to essentials ("Pass the salt" and "Can I have the salad dressing?") for a little while.

Denny finally pushed his bowl away and wiped his mouth with one of the paper napkins Melissa had piled between us. "That was incredible. I'm stuffed."

I nodded while chewing on the end of a drumstick. "It's been my favorite thing since I was little. My mom used to bring me here when I got bored and cranky at the DZ."

"Your mom? Was she there today?"

I shook my head quickly and looked down at the chicken. Suddenly it seemed slimy and lumpy, so I pushed the still half-full bowl over to Denny, who shook his head too. "Couldn't fit it in."

"My mom died when I was six years old," I said quickly, surprised at the tightness in my throat. It's not like I wasn't used to the fact. I looked at my phone, almost hoping my dad would call so I'd have an excuse to end the conversation.

"Sorry."

"Thanks."

"Was she a skydiver?" Denny asked. I liked how he just asked, as though of course I'd want to talk about her. And I did, even though I didn't have much practice. Once a new girl in middle school had asked if my mom would let me go to the movies with her. The teacher took her aside, and when the girl came back she avoided me. I knew I should have felt grateful to the teacher for explaining, but I had wanted to be the one to tell for once. Not necessarily how it had happened, because the thrill factor made it seem like the way she died was more important than the fact that she wasn't around anymore.

I nodded. "She stopped here for a meet on her way to a concert in Kentucky, but she never made it to the concert. She and my dad got married six weeks later."

"Nice."

"And then she and three other women put together a competitive team where they did formation in meets. She was on another team called the SkyWitches, which did demo jumps, like into football games and rock concerts.

So I've already made a bunch of jumps. I just wasn't born yet. She didn't stop until the doctor told her that if she broke her pelvis, it could kill me." I held out my hand. "Let me show you something on your phone." My dad thought smartphones were extravagant and said I'd have to pay for my own if I really wanted one. I'd decided I'd rather save my money for college.

I scrolled through videos. It was oddly exciting to be talking about my mom. Sometimes, longtime jumpers who showed up at the DZ would look at me like they were trying to figure out why I looked familiar, and then when they heard my name I'd see understanding dawn on their faces. Usually they'd get awkward and look away, but I loved it when they said, "Wow, you look just like Jenna!"

I found my favorite SkyWitches video and turned the phone so we could both see the screen. Patsy, Louisa, Michelle, and my mom exited the jump plane at the same time and joined together in a circle, holding hands.

Then they turned on the smoke canisters strapped to their heels and tracked across the sky, still in freefall, in four parallel lines, making brown smoke streaks. Their canopies opened at the same instant. Everything they wore was black—not just the canopies, but the lines, the packs, their jumpsuits—everything, which was dramatic against the blue sky. All that black dye made the rigs really heavy, and they had to be careful where they landed because any dirt they got on the canopies would show. But it was worth it for the effect. Everything being black looked so cool.

"Wow!" Denny's breath was warm on my cheek. I

was suddenly conscious of my messy ponytail, my lack of makeup, the hangar dust under my fingernails. I hoped I didn't smell too sweaty and clamped my elbows down on my sides.

"It gets even better." On the video, the SkyWitches pulled the brooms out of the keepers my dad had sewn onto the legs of their jumpsuits. The broomsticks extended like telescopes, and the SkyWitches snapped them open and tucked them under their legs, bending their knees like they were riding on them, steering their canopies one-handed. My dad had made special steering toggles for that, but Louisa said that even so, steering was the hardest part of the jump. Smoke streamed behind them.

"Surrender Dorothy," Denny said.

I nodded. "Exactly."

The spectators at the football game went wild as the SkyWitches circled overhead under canopy and then came in close. They dropped their brooms an instant before they all did stand-up landings. It was amazing.

Then the camera swung upward. Suddenly you saw what nobody had noticed before because they were watching the SkyWitches: four more skydivers were coming in. One of them was my dad. They wore short vests and tiny hats, and from their shoulders stretched what looked like bat wings.

"Oh wow!" Denny said again. "The Flying Monkeys!"

The four jumpers landed and hopped around the Sky-Witches, who picked up their brooms and chased them out of the stadium. I had seen it dozens of times, and I still loved it.

"That's amazing," Denny said. "How many jumps do you have to make before you can do something like that?" It sounded like he couldn't wait to try it himself. I could understand. The thought of flying like that, so smooth and so precise, was exciting.

"Depends, I guess. A hundred, maybe? If you're really good. Probably more."

Melissa came and cleared the table. "Dessert?"

I shook my head. "I'm stuffed."

"What do you have?" Denny asked. Boys amaze me. They can be full one minute and ready for dessert the next.

Melissa rattled off a list and Denny looked at me. "Chocolate pie," I said. "Trust me. Just coffee for me."

She brought my coffee and a huge slab of pie and two forks. I took a bite, and while Denny finished it, I talked to him about getting off student status, about static line versus AFF, about learning how to track and turn and all the other skills you need in order to do competitive formations and demos.

"So minimum seven AFFs until I solo?" he asked.

I nodded. "And AFF's pretty expensive. Static line is cheaper."

Denny looked out the window. "The expense isn't really an issue."

I looked out too, at the pretty little sports car. "I figured." He turned pink. I'd never known a guy who blushed so easily. I changed the subject hastily. "Old-school jumpers like my dad say static line is the only real way to know if you're up for doing it long term. He says that even in AFF, you have someone there in case something goes wrong, but the very first static-line jump you do, you climb out all alone. That really tests you, he says. But not many people do it, so he's not set up for it."

Denny drummed his fingers on the table. "So I could go someplace else and do a static-line jump?"

It irritated me to realize how much I didn't want him to go to another drop zone, but I nodded.

"Where, do you think?"

"There's another DZ not too far away," I said. "Past Knoxton, just over the county line." He picked up his phone and looked a question at me. "It's called the Jump Ranch."

He tapped on his phone. "Oh right. I looked into that one. I wondered how come there were two drop zones so close together."

"They don't really compete. The Jump Ranch—well, it's more casual, I guess." I didn't want to bad-mouth the competition even though the Ranch was kind of notorious. We'd heard stories about sloppy pack jobs and about jumpers drinking and diving.

"Is it safe to jump there?"

"They have a pretty high injury rate—broken ankles, things like that. No fatalities since one of their aircraft went in a few years ago. Everybody got out but the pilot, but the FAA decided it was his fault, not the DZ's, so they didn't do anything. Norton—one of our pilots who's also a mechanic—he's worked on some of their planes, and he says they're in decent shape."

More finger drumming.

Then Denny said, "I know your dad's place has a good safety record."

"Lowest number of injuries in the state, and one of the best safety records in the country. He got an award from the USPA for that once."

"Any fatalities?"

"Just one." I forced the words through the tightness in my throat. "Just one, ten years ago."

7

Of course Denny wanted details about the one fatality at Skydive Knoxton. I said that it was a long time ago and not the fault of the DZ, not anybody's fault, really, just bad luck, and that my dad didn't like to talk about it. But I figured Denny would probably find it online, and he'd notice that the dead jumper's last name was Clancy. If he read a news report, he'd find out that the Jenna Clancy who went in was the wife of the drop zone's owner, so he'd obviously figure out that she was my mom.

I knew I should tell him myself before he found out on his own. But even though I kept wanting to be the one to tell someone about my mom, when it came right down to it, I couldn't talk about how she died. I was trying to force some words out when the shift-change whistle blew from the paper plant outside of town.

"Oh shoot," I said. "What time is it?"

Denny glanced at his phone. "Three o'clock."

I jumped up. "I've got to get back." My dad would probably let his AFF student take a break around now, and he'd be sure to see I was gone.

Denny insisted on paying for lunch, and Melissa hugged us both good-bye.

"So what's the rush?" Denny asked as we left the few buildings that made up "town" behind us.

"My dad," I said. "He'll worry if he notices I'm gone."

"So call him." I didn't answer, and he glanced over at me. "It's something else, isn't it?"

I looked out the window. "It's hard to explain. He—well, he's overprotective, I guess."

"So if he notices you're gone, he'll freak out?"

I nodded. "He won't actually *do* anything. He'll just worry a lot."

"Huh."

Now it was my turn to glance at him. "What do you mean, 'huh'?"

"Nothing."

"No, really. What did you mean?"

"Not my business. And my mom keeps telling me to keep my amateur psychology to myself."

"Okay, now you *have* to tell me!"

"Well . . ." He hesitated. "I don't know either of you very well, but it sounds like *you're* the overprotective one."

"Oh, come on."

"Like I said, amateur psychology. I don't know what I'm talking about. But most people don't get all panicky when they realize their dad might be worried."

"I'm not . . ." I stopped. *Was* I being overprotective? No, that was silly. "You know not whereof you speak, shrink-in-training."

We pulled into the lot. "Ruh-roh," Denny muttered, à la Scooby-Doo. My dad, looking even taller than his actual six foot two, stood outside the office, punching at his phone. When he saw us he slammed the phone shut and shoved it in his pocket.

"Crap," I said under my breath. I forced a smile as I got out. "Hey, Dad!"

"Where have you been?" he barked.

"Adrienne's. Why? Did you need me? Cynthia said that Randy would pack—"

"That's not the point." He broke off as Denny came up.

"Is something wrong?" Denny looked at me, then at my dad, and then at me again.

My dad's smile looked as phony as mine felt. "Nothing you did. Clancy should have checked with me before leaving the grounds." He made it sound like a prison.

I said, "Sorry. I thought it was enough to tell Cynthia. Next time I'll check out with you personally. Or have you thought about installing a time clock?"

He shot me a look that meant I'd be in trouble if there

hadn't been a customer present, and I took advantage of his forced self-restraint to say, "Thanks for lunch, Denny."

"Okay," Denny said uncertainly. "See you."

I felt their eyes on me as I walked to the hangar. Randy, of course, was nowhere to be seen, and he had barely made a dent in the pile of rigs. No wonder my dad was angry. But it wasn't my fault; it was Randy's. I cussed him out under my breath as I swung the first rig onto the packing table. "Self-centered son of a—"

"C.C." It was my dad.

I didn't answer.

"Clancy." He sounded tired.

I kept on packing until he laid a hand on the slider before I could position it. I whirled around. "*What?*"

"You know what. I don't know that young man. He seems nice, and he's certainly eager to learn to jump, but you shouldn't have gotten in his car without checking with me. I don't know anything about him."

"You don't need to," I muttered.

"What do you mean by that?"

"Nothing." I wiped my nose with the back of my hand, sure I was leaving a black streak on my face. *Whatever.* I turned back to the rig.

"And he let you take the blame for leaving. He should have stood up like a man and said that it was his fault."

"But he didn't know there was anything to take the blame *for!*"

"Young lady—"

I made an exasperated grunt, and he started over.

"Clancy, you don't have a good track record in choosing friends. Remember that girl Miranda who told those lies about—"

I spun on him again. "Miranda? *Miranda*? Dad, that was in elementary school. You can't keep punishing me for Miranda!"

He went on as though I hadn't spoken. "And you wanted to go to the eighth-grade dance with that boy whose brother was in jail."

"Really? The best you can do is come up with things that happened years ago? And what Sammy's brother did wasn't Sammy's fault. He was a nice kid."

He ignored my question. "You were too young to date, anyway. In some ways you still *are* too young, except with someone as responsible as Theo." I was *so* tempted to ask him how old my mom had been when she started to date—she was only nineteen when they got married. Before I could give in to the temptation, he went on. "But I never would have let you go out with a boy from a family with a felon in it. Honey, let's just say that you don't have the best judgment about people."

"Oh no? What about Theo?" I challenged him.

He smiled. "Okay, I'll grant you Theo. Go sit in the office and cool off for a bit. I'll finish this one."

"I can do it," I said, but he stopped me.

"Don't ever pack when you're upset."

"Well, then, don't upset me when I'm packing," I snapped. I stomped out of the hangar and into the office. When I was in middle school and we had a fight, I used to write MAD AT DAD on my hand so I wouldn't forget and be nice to him by accident. But these days I didn't need any reminders.

Noel and Leon were in the lounge and I didn't feel like talking to anyone, not even them, so I went to the office and sat on one of the folding chairs along the wall. A bunch of students milled around. I gathered they'd been waiting to get rigged up for a while and were starting to wonder what was taking so long. I would *kill* Randy the next time I saw him. I held a *Jump!* magazine in front of my face so no one would talk to me.

Cynthia called a load and most of the students disappeared. I pulled out my phone and texted Theo: See you tonight?

No answer. He must have been on duty. But why hadn't he texted me during a break? Surely he'd have had at least one by now. He always texted me during his breaks. Maybe he'd forgotten to charge his phone.

I found a text from Denny, though, with a link to his jump video, which I opened on Cynthia's computer when she took a bathroom break. He didn't look at all dorky. He looked—well, he looked pretty hot, if anyone can look hot with the wind slamming them around and with huge goggles covering half their face.

My dad would be going up in the next load with his AFF student, so the coast was clear in the hangar. Cynthia came back, and I went in and packed the rest of the rigs, listening to my iPod so my brain would be occupied.

The AFF went well and the student said she was going

to sign up for the full course. A few loads of tandems went up, and then Cynthia called a load of fun jumpers who were celebrating the seventieth birthday of one of them. I took a break and went outside to watch them land. Nobody has more fun than skydivers who've been jumping for decades, even though they always spend a lot of time saying how much the sport has changed since the eighties (good thing, too, my dad always says), and my mood finally improved when I saw how happy they were.

And then my mood improved even more. A familiar voice called my name, and I turned around.

"Angie!" I shrieked.

"Hey, baby!" She wrapped me in her arms.

People were always surprised when I told them that of all the SkyWitches—Angie, Patsy, Michelle, and Louisa—Angie was the one who had taken my mother's place the most. She was lean and hard-bodied, not warm and cuddly like you'd imagine a substitute mom. But while I was close to all of them, Angie was the one who told me about periods and where babies come from, and she helped me buy new clothes when I got tired of the T-shirts and jeans I always wore to the DZ. And she always gave me exactly the right present on my birthday, usually something I hadn't even known I wanted until I opened it.

"How's Leanne?" I asked.

"Still crying over that loser." I didn't know Leanne's husband, Jesse, very well, but he had never gotten along with Angie.

She walked arm-in-arm with me to the hangar.

"Are you back for good or just visiting?"

She popped a piece of nicotine gum in her mouth. She'd quit smoking when her kids were little, but now she was addicted to the gum. "I'm just in town for a couple of days. I came for Jackson's jump."

I hadn't seen her son since he'd left for Vanderbilt, where he had a full scholarship.

"He's jumping?" I asked.

Angie nodded. "Tandem. I told him I could get a discount on an AFF but he wasn't interested." She sat down on the packing table. "So how are things?"

I told Angie about how my dad was loosening up just a teeny bit, letting me drive at the DZ and into Knoxton, and she high-fived me. I also told her about how Theo was getting on my nerves and how I seemed to be getting on his. She didn't like Theo much—she never said why, just that I could "do better"—but she listened without comment, letting me finally get some things off my chest. I knew I was safe with her; I could say bad things about Theo to blow off steam and she wouldn't use them against me later, to try to convince me to dump him.

Cynthia's voice came over the PA system: "Sean, Carla, Josh, Kenny, and"—a dramatic pause—"*Jackson*, go to the hangar." It always made the DZ staff proud to see a kid of one of their own do a first jump.

Jackson smiled at me shyly as Randy rigged him up. I hadn't seen him in a long time and hardly recognized him. I rigged up the girl, Carla, who was chirpy and excited. Their instructors came out and ran through the instructions one more time, and then they all trooped out, nervously tightening and loosening their goggle straps.

"Have fun, kiddo!" Angie called after Jackson. A few parents and friends of the other jumpers also yelled things at them over the sudden noise of the engine. None of them looked as relaxed as Angie did, which wasn't surprising.

The plane taxied out and climbed to altitude really quickly. Norton always did that to be kind to first-jump students, since he knew they didn't want to spend any longer in the plane than they had to. Plus, the longer the ride took, the more chance of someone getting nervous enough to back out and cost my dad some money. He gave a fifty percent refund to anyone who changed their mind. He always said he didn't want anyone to feel pressured into doing something they weren't ready for because they were afraid of losing money.

While we waited, Angie caught up the rest of the regulars on Leanne's situation. "Any idea where Jesse is now?" Randy asked, and Angie shook her head. I'd been so happy to have her to unload on that it hadn't even occurred to me to find out how she was. I resolved to fix that as soon as Jackson was on the ground. She must have been worried about Leanne. And no matter how much she loved her grandchildren, I couldn't see her moving to New Mexico for good. At least I hoped she wouldn't.

"There's the cut," someone said, and the whuffos looked nervous.

"Cut? What are they cutting?" one dad asked, and while someone explained about slowing down the engine, the first tandem came out, followed closely by the second. The plane circled and the other two exited.

"Which one is Jackson?" I asked Angie.

"Your dad said he'd put him out last. He's with Leon."

The other spectators exclaimed about how fast they were falling. One said she was praying, and another asked nervously how long it would be before their parachutes opened, and another said he didn't see why anyone would jump out of a perfectly good airplane.

"It's okay," Angie said. "Everyone's doing just fine."

"You wouldn't be so calm if you had a child up there!" the praying woman said.

"She does," I said.

"What's Jackson going to major in?" Noel asked, ignoring the whuffo.

Angie shaded her eyes with her hand. "He says engineering, but I notice the only class he's talked about is philosophy."

The praying woman looked from one of them to the other as though they were crazy to be talking about majors and philosophy while their loved ones were falling to the earth at more than one hundred miles per hour.

One by one, the tandems landed. Randy even managed a stand-up landing with his student because the student was so short there was no chance his feet would touch the ground before Randy's. Jackson and Leon landed last. They slid a bit on the grass before jumping up. Jackson's face was split in a huge grin, and he hugged Angie hard after gathering up his gear. "I guess I can forgive you for spending all that time out here when I was a kid if it's always that much fun!" he said.

"Trust me," she answered. "The more you do it, the more fun it is."

Mad Jack trotted up, still wearing his camera helmet. "Hey, Angie! You making a jump?"

"You bet. My rig's in the car. Be right back."

After making two jumps, Angie said she had to go home, but she promised we'd get together before she left. She waved out the car window as she peeled out of the parking lot.

Now that the days were so long, I was starving by the time Dad and I left the DZ. I kept my earbuds in so I wouldn't have to talk until we stopped for dinner on the way home. I was surprised to look up and see that we were in the parking lot of a new Thai place. Dad doesn't like Thai and I love it, so stopping there was a kind of peace offering.

"Going out with Theo when we get home?" Dad asked. I shook my head. I had texted Theo again before we left the DZ, and he still hadn't answered. I texted Julia and asked if she'd seen him but she said no. A few minutes later she texted again and said that Justin thought he was busy doing something for his mom. Huh. Theo hadn't mentioned that.

When we got home, I let myself in the house while Dad took stacks of order forms and a bundle of nylon out of the trunk. During the week, when he wasn't at the DZ, he repaired and customized rigs and made new ones to order.

I closed myself in my room. I had long ago taken down

the sign on the door that warned of excruciating punishment if anyone came in, as my dad had finally learned that my room was off limits. I opened my art history book, but my mind wandered until I gave up.

I pulled my laptop over and googled "leukemia." It turned out there were lots of different kinds, and I wondered which one Frederick had. It looked like childhood leukemia was a lot more curable than the kind adults get. Did a teenager count as a child or an adult?

My phone pinged and I leaped on it. A text from Theo, finally. Home yet?

I texted back: Just got in. You?

Theo: At Macks with J & J. Want to come?

Yay! He asked instead of just telling me he was coming to pick me up. Mack's was a burger place near Julia's house. I wrote back: Sure. Come get me?

A pause. Finally he answered.

Theo: Aren't you too tired?

A longer pause. Me: Ok never mind

I held down the power button until the phone turned off, and flopped onto my bed. What was going on? Theo asked me if I wanted to go out and then acted all surprised when I said yes. Maybe my dad was right that texting was a bad way to communicate.

Or maybe Theo was sure I'd say no and that he'd get good-boyfriend points for asking me, but for some reason he didn't want to see me. He was having too good a time, maybe, or he didn't want to drive all the way to my house. A little voice in me said, *He might be out with another girl.*

But then I scolded myself. One, Theo wouldn't cheat on me, and two, he knew that Julia would kill him if he showed up with someone else. I was being paranoid and ridiculous.

I turned my phone back on and called his number.

He didn't answer.

8

FACT: When a skydiver experiences a "first"—first reserve ride, first night jump, first jump with a new rig, first competition jump, etc.—tradition requires her to buy a case of beer for her fellow jumpers. As a result, skydivers avoid using the word "first" in reference to any aspect of jumping, no matter how small, for fear that witnesses will demand a case of beer.

—The Whuffo's Guide to Skydiving

I woke up a few times that night. I didn't know what was going on—I had made Theo mad or something, and he wouldn't tell me why. He would never talk about it when things weren't good. Julia always said Theo was a typical male and not to worry when he wouldn't communicate. I didn't believe that all males were like that, and I wasn't worried. I was frustrated.

Finally, I gave up on sleep and went to the kitchen. I drank a mug of coffee while the sun came up, my textbook open on the table in front of me. I couldn't read a word. And then of course I started feeling sleepy just as soon as it was time to catch the bus to meet Julia at the salon. My dad had left a ten-dollar bill on the counter with a note saying *Get yourself a haircut too, if you want. My treat.* Clearly, he had no idea what a haircut cost these days, but it was still nice of him.

A familiar car was idling in front of the bus stop. Julia. I ran up to the window, which she lowered with a grin. "Just happened to be in the neighborhood," she said. "Need a lift?"

"You're *evil!*" I let myself in.

A lidded paper coffee cup stood in the cup holder between the seats. I knew it would have extra milk and two sugars, just how I liked it. I was happy that Julia had thought of it. *There's a difference between being thoughtful and taking care of someone who doesn't need it*, I told myself.

"Why didn't you tell me you were going to pick me up?" I asked as she pulled out. The feeling of triumph over fooling my dad was so exhilarating that it squelched the little bit of guilt I felt about getting into Julia's car.

"I was afraid you'd say no."

"Why would I—" I stopped, but Julia answered my unspoken question.

"You'd say that if your dad found out, he'd get all upset. I figured once I was here you'd come along."

I took a sip of coffee. "He would, you know. He's getting more like a fascist all the time."

"He isn't *that* bad," Julia said sharply.

I looked at her, surprised. "He's not?" She'd always sympathized with my complaints about my dad and his strictness before.

She kept her eyes on the road, but her fingers were clamped tight to the steering wheel. "At least he cares. At least he's around. It's better to be too protective than not to give a shit." She wiped the back of her hand across her nose. She stopped at a red light.

"Jules . . ." I gave her a tissue. "It has purse crumbs on it, but it's clean."

She blew her nose. "It's just that it was Celia's birthday yesterday"—Celia was her little sister—"and Daddy didn't even call or send her a card or anything. She didn't cry, but she was really sad."

Poor Celia. Sometimes she was a drama queen, but that must have really hurt.

"He's such an ass," she muttered.

"I'm sorry, Jules."

She nodded, the light turned green, and we moved on. We didn't say anything more about it—we didn't need to.

"Oh, guess what?" I said. "Angie's here!"

"For good?" Julia sounded excited—she was crazy about Angie.

"Just a few days. Jackson made a jump, so she came here for that. I think she also needed a break from Leanne and the twins."

"I don't blame her," Julia said. Being with kids at the miniature-golf place must have been getting old.

"So how was Mack's?" I asked after a while.

"Good. After, we went to a party at Jacob's house. Danced a lot."

"Theo too?"

"Uh-huh." I could hardly understand her through the yawn.

"What time did you get back?"

"One thirty? Two? Something like that."

We stopped at a light, waiting to turn into the mall, when Julia asked out of the blue, "Are you and Theo okay?"

I glanced at her, but her eyes were fixed on the stoplight. "Yeah, sure. Why?"

She shrugged as the light turned green, and she waited until she could turn left. A gap in the oncoming traffic appeared and she gunned the engine. Brakes squealed and horns blared, but she didn't seem to notice. "Jules, be careful!" I said.

"Oh, they were overreacting. There was plenty of room." She scanned the lot for a space.

"Why did you ask if everything was good with me and Theo?" I asked. "Did he say something?" I didn't want to tell her that it felt like he'd been avoiding me. I looked out the window and tried to sound casual. "Was he dancing with someone else?"

"Nobody more than once, except me when Justin got tired. But it was strange that we were out without you." She pulled into a space barely ahead of a car that was waiting with its blinker on. The driver yelled something, but she ignored him.

"I was at the DZ all day, and I was exhausted. You don't know how hard it is to pack parachutes for twelve hours." I sounded defensive and accusatory, maybe because I agreed that it was strange that Theo had gone dancing without me.

"There's no reason Theo can't go out when I'm busy. It's not like we're married."

As we got out of the car, Julia looked at my hair. "Sure you don't want a haircut?" she asked. "All I'm getting is a trim, so Bethany will probably have time to do you too. I can pay for you. My mom's paying for mine, and I have tons of birthday money left."

I was tired of feeling like the poor relation. "Okay. If she has time, she can cut my hair too. But I'm paying." I refused to think about the dent that this would make in my college fund.

Bethany did have time. She was cute and funny, and she knew some of our friends through her younger brother Thomas, who was in our grade. A sign with prices for different services was posted on the wall. It was even more expensive than I'd guessed, so when I had been shampooed and was sitting in Bethany's chair, I said firmly, "Just a cut, please."

She stood behind me, combing out my wet hair with her head tilted to one side. "Same thing? Or maybe try something new?"

"Clancy has a hard time trying anything new," Julia said.

"Usually I do," I agreed, "but maybe this time . . ." I studied my face as Bethany played with my hair, looping it up to see what it would be like shorter, pulling it off my face. "What about something that would make me look older?"

"Like what?" Julia asked.

I hesitated, and then, before I could lose my nerve, I said, "Whatever Bethany wants to do. As long as it's just a cut, no color or anything." I added the last part hastily, before the dye pots and other mysterious things came out and depleted my bank account even more.

Bethany turned my back to the mirror so it would be a surprise and told Julia not to say anything. As she combed and cut, and she and Julia joked around, I regretted more and more that I had put myself at a stranger's mercy. *Hair grows, hair grows*, I told myself over and over again while the scissors made that clean snipping sound.

Bethany pulled out the blow-dryer and I said, "No, thanks." I started to get up, but Bethany pushed me back. "Styling's included when you allow the stylist to experiment. I need to see the final result so I know how I did."

She was probably just being nice, but I didn't stop her. She blew my hair with hot air, brushing it out, and finally stopped and undid the plastic cape. "Ready?"

I nodded. She turned me around so I could see myself.

Julia said, "Finally! I thought I was going to burst! You look *great*, Clance!"

Did I? I looked so different, I couldn't tell whether it was good or bad. My hair was a lot shorter, barely long enough for a ponytail, and she had cut bangs that swooped down the sides of my face and made me look like I had cheekbones. The ends were wispier than the blunt cut I'd had before.

"What do you think?" Bethany sounded anxious. "Do you think you look older?"

I nodded. I really did. But I couldn't speak, because I suddenly realized what people meant when they said I looked like my mom. She had long hair in the snapshots that Mad Jack had taken of her and my dad getting married, but she cut it off right after that—long hair gets all tangled in freefall, even with a helmet. In my memories of her, she always had short hair.

"Think this will make your dad treat you like a big girl now?" Julia asked.

"Oh, overprotective dad?" Bethany asked. "I feel your pain. Mine would still get me a babysitter if I let him. He lets Tommy do all sorts of things I could never do at his age."

I tipped Bethany more than I could afford. I glanced at the mirror once more before we went back out into the sunshine of the parking lot. The haircut was less of a shock this time since I knew what to expect, and it looked good. I hoped.

"Look, there's Theo." Julia waved and Theo waved back from his car.

Suddenly I was nervous about seeing him. "Come say hi," I said to Julia, but she shook her head.

"See you!" she called as she trotted to her car.

I slid into Theo's passenger seat. He leaned over and gave me a kiss, and I realized how ridiculous I was being. He hadn't been ignoring my texts. He had just been busy, that was all.

Right, a busy lifeguard. I told my little internal voice to shut up.

I realized that Theo wasn't moving. "What do you think?" I turned my head a little so he could get the full effect.

He started the car and put it in gear. "It's nice," he said without enthusiasm.

"It's okay—you don't have to like it." I squeezed his knee. "I think it will take some getting used to."

"You know I'd think you were beautiful even if you shaved your head," he said, and I said, "Wish I'd known that before! I could have shaved it myself for nothing."

He laughed, and then everything was normal. We went to Manuelito's for a taco and then to the park next to the elementary school. Theo pulled some sodas out of a small backpack and passed me one.

"What a Boy Scout," I said. "Always prepared."

He flashed his killer smile. "You have no idea," he said, but then refused to tell me what he meant. He opened the bottles, we drank the soda, and we swung on the swings. I snagged the one that was strung the highest and swung higher than he did because he had to keep his long legs stuck straight out in front of him. He gave up trying to beat me and hopped off at the top of his swing, landing like a cat. He stood in front of me, grinning. I slid off into his arms, which were waiting for me, steady and reliable, just like I knew they'd be. We sat on a bench and kissed for a long time.

After a while Theo stood, drawing me up with him. He nuzzled my neck, then pulled away slightly.

"Let's go for a walk." His voice was husky. He tilted his head toward the path that led to the passion pit that every high-school freshman class thought was their secret until they heard their parents talking about it nostalgically.

It was just a dip in the ground, surrounded by scruffy trees. Empty beer cans were always strewn around it, but you'd have thought it was the most romantic spot in town, the way people talked. It was where Julia had lost her virginity to Justin, and I knew that they went back every once in a while, and not just for nostalgia's sake. I had never been there with Theo, or with any other boy, for that matter.

I held back. "Theo . . ."

"Don't worry. I only want some privacy." He kissed me again. "You know I'd never hurt you."

That was kind of creepy. Until he said that, I wasn't worried about being hurt. I was worried about being pressured. I had no plans to sleep with Theo. I'd figured out long ago that my mom was pregnant with me when she and my dad got married. I don't know if she was planning to marry him anyway or if she wanted to go to college or do something else instead, but I wasn't about to make the same mistake. Not that I'd stay a virgin forever, but being married and having a baby wasn't on my to-do list for a while yet.

Dr. Mike, a psychologist Angie had convinced my dad to take me to, told me that many children of people who died young were superstitious that they were fated to die young too, and that sometimes they even thought they were kind of a reincarnation of their dead parent, especially if they were the same gender. Sometimes I did feel like that.

I told myself I was being stupid, and the thought of getting out of the harsh sun and into the cool darkness was nice, so I allowed Theo to lead me through the trees. The unwritten but well-known laws of the passion pit said first come, first served and no spying. I didn't know if I hoped or feared that someone else would be there ahead of us. But it was vacant.

Theo opened his backpack. He pulled out a quilt and spread it on the ground. "Boy Scout!" I teased again. Something about my body chemistry made me irresistible to chiggers, and if there was even one in the grass, it would be sure to bite me someplace I couldn't scratch in public. *How sweet of Theo to remember that and bring the quilt.*

Theo reached for me. I said, "Wait a minute" and silenced my phone, and then I opened my arms and he scooped me up off my feet. He lowered us both down until we were stretched full length on the quilt.

"Theo—" I began.

"It's okay," he said. "I'll stop as soon as you say. I promise."

So I made no objection when Theo's hand went up my back and he undid my bra, and I even guided his hand around to my front, where he cupped my breast and then lowered his mouth to it. His tongue was so soft and his teeth so sharp that I felt an inward tug from where his mouth was all the way down to my belly, and I kissed the top of his head and slid my hand down, unzipping his jeans. I squeezed his butt, pulling him against me.

He sat up and drew me onto his lap, facing him. I straddled his thighs and put my hands on his broad shoulders, looking into his dark eyes. He was so handsome. I kissed him, long and slowly, and put his hand back on my breast. "Don't," he groaned, but I kissed him harder until our teeth clicked, and he put his other hand down the back of my jeans.

"Theo," I whispered, involuntarily lifting my hips a little.

This was where I usually pulled away, but this time Theo leaned back and thrust his free hand into his back pocket. He took something out that glinted metallically in the light coming through the leaves. Before I could say anything, his mouth was on mine, and he was kissing me again. Then he was licking my earlobe and his hand was at my waistband, unbuttoning my shorts. I felt butterflies, not just in my stomach, but everywhere from my lap to my throat, and I couldn't get enough of him.

He was doing something with whatever he had pulled out of his pocket. I blinked, focusing my eyes, and sure enough, it was a condom packet.

Suddenly, the butterflies went away.

"I love you, Clancy," Theo whispered. "And you love me. You do, don't you?"

I nodded.

"Say it," he said.

"I love you, Theo," I murmured. "I love you so much, but—"

Abruptly he sat up. "But?"

With that one tiny word I had ruined it. "But I'm just—just not ready, I guess."

He tried to smile. "Don't you want your first time to be with someone who loves you? Someone who wants you to be happy?"

I sat up too and put my arms around his neck. I stared at him, at his beautiful dark eyes, at his mouth, swollen from our kissing.

"I *do* want my first time to be with you," I whispered. "But not now. Not here." I looked at the beer cans, the cigarette butts, the fast-food wrappers.

He put his arm around me and drew me close to nestle against his chest. "It's okay," he whispered, but his voice was thick with disappointment.

"Maybe we could kind of . . . " I felt relieved that he was being nice about it and didn't seem too disappointed, but it was so awkward that I didn't know what to say. "We could kind of work up to it. We have all summer."

I started to kiss him again, but he drew back.

"I need to tell you something," he said quietly.

9

Waveoff (or *wave-off*): A signal to other jumpers in freefall that you are about to deploy your parachute. This warns them to move out of your area to avoid a collision.

—*The Whuffo's Guide to Skydiving*

Uh-oh. No good conversation ever started with "I need to tell you something."

My mouth went dry and I tried to hide my worry. "Okay. What?" Was he breaking up with me? Was this my choice—have sex with him or be dumped?

He took a deep breath. "Over the winter I applied for a job at a summer camp. I didn't tell you because I never thought I'd get it, and I was right—I didn't. But one of the counselors came down with mono, and no one else but me is available to fill in at short notice."

My relief that he wasn't breaking up with me made this

seem unimportant, but then I realized what he was saying. "So you got the job after all?"

He nodded.

"Is this a day camp?" I knew it wasn't, or he wouldn't be making such a big production out of telling me.

He shook his head. "Sleepaway."

"Where is it?"

"Idaho."

I sat up straighter. "*Idaho?*"

He nodded again.

I stared at him. "So . . . you figured that this was your last chance this summer to sleep with me?"

"Oh, come on, Clancy! You know that's not it. I wanted to give us something to remember when we're far apart, something to make us feel close—"

"You need something to *make* you feel close to me?"

"Clancy." He stopped and then said, without looking at me, "Why are you being like this? It's like you're mad at me all the time."

"All—"

"Okay, not *all* the time. But a lot of the time. I just thought that this"—he waved his hand vaguely—"would bring us closer together."

I didn't know what to say. What *could* I say? *Oh, now that I know you're going, well then, sure! Where'd that condom get to?*

"Wrong, huh?" He didn't sound hurt or mad, just—rueful, I guess, and I scooted closer. He put his arm around me and I leaned into him, smelling the familiar Theo smell.

"Maybe the timing was off." It was the best I could do.

Julia once said that guys use sex to get closer to someone, but girls need to be close to someone to have sex. I usually disagreed when she made such sweeping statements, but maybe this time she was right.

He said into my hair, "I had to tell you today. I have to leave really soon."

I kissed his cheek. That must have encouraged him, because he went on eagerly, "It's one of the best camps in the country. Outdoor adventures. It's in a very remote place. They don't have internet or cell service. The counselors have walkie-talkies in case of emergencies, but that's all. They want me to teach rock climbing, and it's not on an artificial wall, but on cliffs. There's white-water kayaking and caving and—"

I said carefully, trying to sound curious and not accusatory, "Why didn't you tell me before?"

"I just said. I knew they wouldn't offer me the job. They give preference to people who went to camp there, and they told me that there probably weren't going to be any openings for people who didn't."

"But if you applied for it, you must have at least hoped that . . ." I couldn't go on.

"I don't get it." He really did sound confused. "What difference does it make? Are you saying that if you'd known, you'd have applied for a job there too so we could be together? You don't have any outdoor skills—"

"Is that all they do? Outdoor skills? Don't they have regular camp stuff too? Remember when I helped Julia put on that play with her day-care kids? I could—"

"No, just outdoor skills. Rock climbing, kayaking, caving, that kind of thing."

Of course I'd never done any of those things. My dad would have flipped.

"And anyway, you're always talking about that class you're taking." He sounded resentful.

"It's important to me, Theo. If I get just a few AP credits before I graduate," I said for what felt like the hundredth time, "I can finish college in seven semesters. And if I take a heavy course load my first two years, I might be able to do it in three years. That would save me *a lot* of money."

"I've told you I don't like it when you talk to me like I'm an idiot." He was trying to make *me* feel like the bad one.

"Sorry, sir," I said with mock humility. "I will attempt to use a tone that you find acceptable. Is this okay, sir?"

"You know it isn't," he growled, and he stood up so suddenly that I flinched. He stomped off toward his car. I stared after him in disbelief and with a pang of guilt. I had to admit that I had been pretty obnoxious. Was I over-reacting to his announcement? Lots of couples spent the summer apart, after all. It wasn't that big a deal.

But then lots of them broke up in the fall. The thought gave me a chill. Was I really to blame for this by taking a silly class?

By not sleeping with him?

I knew Theo would be waiting for me in his car. He would never leave me to walk the mile and a half to my house. So I cut over a block and headed for home that way. The sidewalk blurred through my tears.

One Friday when I was in third or fourth grade, my dad didn't get a memo about school being a half day, and he didn't come to pick me up. I wasn't allowed to ride the school bus ever since a kid had been hit by a car after getting off it. I didn't want the teachers to see me all alone and make a big deal about it. They already fussed over me because I didn't have a mother, and I hated it. I didn't have a cell phone yet, and it didn't occur to me to ask the office to call him. So I decided to walk home. It had always seemed such a short distance in a car, but walking took a lot longer than I'd expected. By the time I saw my dad driving toward me, his face all panicky, I was exhausted.

I felt the same now—abandoned, and far from home.

I hadn't even made it two blocks when Theo pulled up next to me. "Get in, Clancy," he said. "Please."

"I feel like walking." I kept going.

"Come on."

I ignored him. I heard him park and the car door slam. Then he was standing on the sidewalk, blocking my way. I stopped and looked up at his dark eyes, framed by thick lashes. Before I knew it, we were hugging in the middle of the sidewalk, and I let him lead me back to his car.

"It'll be fine," he said. "It's only eight weeks. I'll be going to town for supplies once in a while, and I'll call or text you then."

Oh right. No cell or internet at the camp.

"You'll be so busy you won't even notice I'm gone," he went on.

I stared out the window at the familiar neighborhood

going by. He still didn't get it. I'd miss him—of course I would. But he had just sprung it on me, like my opinion didn't matter, like I would automatically be okay with whatever he wanted to do. That was the real problem. That, and knowing that he would be doing something new and adventurous while I was at the DZ, where I'd spent most of my life, packing rigs, playing with Ripstop, listening to shoulda-died stories. Up till this moment I'd been fine with that, but now I felt like a hamster on a wheel. I couldn't say this to Theo, not right before he left for weeks. I'd already come close to ruining everything.

"It'll be fine," I echoed him. I was too tired of it all to argue anymore. "Sounds like a great camp." I turned to him and made myself smile.

"It is." He pulled up in front of my house and turned off the engine.

"What are you doing?" I asked.

"Coming in." He sounded surprised.

I got out. "Too much homework. Sorry." I couldn't listen to Theo tell my dad about the camp and pretend to be fine with it. I'd burst.

"But, Clancy, I'm leaving—"

"Sorry," I repeated. I climbed the porch steps and let myself in.

Inside, my dad was sitting at the sewing machine, making a custom canopy. Purple-and-green nylon swirled around him.

"There you are!" He cut a thread and put his scissors down. "I was just about to call."

"We went to the park," I said. I walked over and fingered the garish fabric. "Someone wants to be visible." I tried to sound natural, but I must not have succeeded because he stretched and swiveled his chair around.

He looked up at me without saying anything, an odd expression on his face. Oh right—the haircut. "Like it?" I asked, turning around so he could get the full effect.

"A lot." He cleared his throat and turned back to his work. "Where's Theo? Didn't he come in with you?"

"He had to go." I went into the kitchen before he could ask anything else. I didn't want to have to tell him that Theo was leaving for the rest of the summer, and that I hadn't known anything about it until just now. I knew I'd start crying, and I didn't want to deal with explaining right now. And if I did explain, my dad would think I was crying because I was going to miss my boyfriend, when really it would be because I was hurt and angry.

I didn't even feel like calling Angie. It seemed like I was always whining to her.

I remembered that my phone was silenced, and I glanced at it. I had a text from Denny: Monkey poop smells worse than you'd even think.

I felt myself smile as I wrote back: How do you know how badly I think?

Denny, after a long pause: Hey I thought you were ignoring me

Me: Phone silenced. Sorry about the monkey poop

Denny: It's seriously not good. But the job looks ok. Nice people

Me: How's F?

Denny: Don't know yet. Dr said he'd be really bad for a while and then he'd either get better or not but the being bad part was going to happen either way

As I tried to think how to answer that, Denny wrote: I just told my parents about buying the whole aff package. They think I'm nuts. Am I?

Me: Not unless my dad and lots of other people are nuts

Denny: See you out there?

Before I could write See you, another text appeared. It was Theo: Need to talk

Wait a second. Another "need to talk"? Theo wouldn't break up with me over the phone. Would he? And anyway, he had just said he loved me.

I texted Denny: See you Saturday. Biting my lip, I went into my room and closed the door. I took two deep breaths and then called Theo.

"Hey." His voice was warm and my tension relaxed just a tiny bit.

"Hey."

"Something's come up," he said. "The camp just called."

I closed my eyes in relief. They didn't need him after all. He was going to spend the summer here, being a lifeguard. But he continued, "One of the other counselors is on her way there, and her car broke down in the middle of nowhere. She's staying in a motel, and they need me to leave tomorrow to pick her up."

I'd had to switch so fast from imagining Theo dumping me, to imagining Theo staying home all summer, to Theo leaving tomorrow that I couldn't speak.

"Clancy? You there?"

I managed to say, "Why you? Why can't someone else—"

"She's right on my way, and I'd have to leave the next day anyway. I have to get trained before the campers come on Saturday. Everyone else is already at the camp, except me and that girl."

Silence.

"Clance?"

"I'm here."

More silence. Then he said, "It'll go fast, you'll see. You'll be so busy with your class and the DZ and everything."

I didn't agree with him but didn't want to spend our last day arguing, so we talked a little bit longer, and he said he'd swing by on his way out of town in the morning to say good-bye. Then he said he had to go pack, and that was it.

I stared at my phone. My summer had been all planned—taking an art history class, hanging out at the pool with Theo, doing things with Julia, spending weekends at the DZ. And now there was a big hole in the "hanging out with Theo" part.

"Clance?" My dad was outside my door. "Can I come in?"

"Uh-huh."

He opened the door and poked his head in. "You okay?"

"Uh-huh."

"Was that Theo?"

"Yup."

"You sure you're feeling okay?" When I didn't answer, he said, "You came home so early, so I wondered—"

"Theo has to get up early tomorrow."

"First shift at the pool?"

I might as well get it over with. I came out and sat with him in the den. He muted the TV and I told him about Theo's job and how he had to leave first thing to drive to Idaho. Of course I didn't tell him about the passion pit. For a second I thought it would serve him right if I did—he'd have to admit that I had made a good decision, despite all the times he tried to convince me that I never did. But the knowledge that Saint Theodore had even thought of it would be enough to make him lock me up until I was twenty-one.

My dad listened until I stopped talking, and then he whistled. "You okay with this?"

"It's not like I have any choice."

"Aw, don't be like that, C.C.," he said. "This is a much better job than lifeguarding." He sounded uncertain, like he was trying to convince himself as much as me, and it suddenly occurred to me that maybe he'd hover even more without Saint Theo around. *Great. Just great.*

"I know. That's not the point." Of course he didn't ask what the point was, and after a minute he turned the sound back on. We watched the newspeople wrapping things up.

My dad switched off the TV and stood and stretched, his fingertips nearly touching the ceiling. He gave me a quick hug. "Absence makes the heart grow fonder, you know."

"Out of sight, out of mind," I countered.

He laughed. "I don't think Theo's about to forget you. Sweet dreams."

That night I lay in bed and stared at the ceiling. "It'll be all right," I whispered.

But would it?

10

Theo came by before my dad was even up. I was dressed and waiting for him on the porch. I acted cheery and told him to have a great time, and he kissed me so sweetly that it almost loosed the tears I was holding back. He waved out the window as he drove away. At the stop sign, he tapped the brake three times to make the lights say "I. Love. You." Then he was gone.

My dad dropped me off at the dentist for a checkup after breakfast. When I came out, carrying the little plastic bag with the tiny plastic floss dispenser and a toothbrush, he was waiting for me in the parking lot.

"Julia could have picked me up." I didn't even try to hide my irritation.

"I don't mind coming to get you."

I do, I thought. "Or you could leave me the car and I could drive myself both ways," I said without much hope, and sure enough, he shook his head. "So you're going to drive me around the rest of my life?"

"You're not an experienced enough driver. It's not like you can dirt dive a car accident to practice what to do ahead of time."

"So how am I supposed to get experience? Plus the state of Missouri thinks I'm competent. They gave me a driver's license." These were both old arguments and I thought I knew what my dad was going to say next, but he surprised me.

"Tell you what. While we're at the DZ, you can be the driver if I need something in Knoxton or if someone lands off and needs to be picked up. Once you're used to driving in the country, we'll talk about driving in the city. How would that be?"

"Really, Dad?" I was so excited that I didn't remind him that Hawkins, Missouri, hardly counted as a city.

"Sure. And instead of paying you per pack job, I'll pay you per hour so you won't lose money if you stop packing to run an errand."

I leaned across the gearshift and kissed him on the cheek. "Thanks, Dad." *Progress!*

My phone pinged and I pulled it out of my purse. "You know you won't be able to do that while you're driving," my dad said.

"Duh! I'm not an idiot!"

Theo had sent me a picture of a skyline with a text saying Kansas City. I replied: Call me when you stop for the night xoxoxoxo

I leaned back, savoring my minor victory. I'd finally have some time to myself on the weekends, even if it was only when I made a run to the hardware store or picked up a stranded jumper.

My dad made the funny little throat-clearing noise he always made when he didn't know how to say something.

"Fear not to speak, revered parent," I said.

"Do you need to go straight home?"

I narrowed my eyes and looked at him. *Why was he acting nervous?* "Not really. Why?"

"While you were inside getting tortured by the dentist, I texted Elise. Her office is just around the corner. She said to bring you by and we'd go out for coffee together."

"What, she wants me to go on your date?"

"It's not a date, Clancy. It's just coffee. Besides, she specifically said to bring you along. She likes you."

We went out to a café near where Elise worked. It turned out they had excellent croissants—my favorite—and I had a pretty good time. Elise was taking a poetry-writing class online, so we talked a little about taking a class with no classroom.

"What kind of work do you do?" I asked, eyeing a third croissant. Elise pushed it over to me and watched me smear butter on it without trying to hide her smile. I knew what she was thinking.

"My record's five," I said, "but I'm out of training right now."

"I was the same way at her age," my dad said. "I could eat a pizza, then go to a friend's for dinner and eat so much I'd embarrass myself."

"I'm a paralegal," Elise said, answering the question I had asked before my appetite became the topic du jour. We talked about that for a while, and then Elise said she had to go back to work. I pretended to be busy retying my shoe while my dad kissed her good-bye. It didn't bother me to see him kiss someone, but he always acted shy about PDAs in front of me. Julia thought that was cute.

"I like her," I said while buckling my seat belt a little later.

"Me too." My dad didn't add anything, but peeking at him from the corner of my eye, I saw that his neck was pink. Huh. I sat back. Of course he liked her if he was still seeing her, but the way he blushed meant something new. Maybe he was finally getting serious about someone. When I was little I used to wish he'd marry Angie, but after a while I realized that wasn't going to happen.

"Sooo . . ." I drew out the word because I didn't know what I'd say after it. "Do you think you'll—do you think the two of you will—I mean, stay together for a while?"

"I don't know." He sounded so uncomfortable that he was making *me* uncomfortable, and I would have changed the subject if I hadn't been so curious.

"She's not really like Mom," I said cautiously. I hoped my comment wouldn't make him stop talking.

He gave a little snort. "No, not at all."

"You sound like that's a good thing," I said. "Like it's good that she's not like Mom."

He was silent for so long that I thought I had gone too far. Then he said, "There never was anyone else like your mother, and there never will be again." And although what he said wasn't an answer, this time I knew I should shut up.

Angie was going back to New Mexico the next morning, so she came by and took me to Manuelito's. I told her about Theo leaving suddenly but made it sound like I was okay with it. I didn't usually fool Angie, but I was pretty sure she believed me. She had a lot on her mind, what with Leanne and Jesse and their kids, after all. If she'd really been my mother, she probably would have picked up on the fact that I was far from okay with it. Or I guessed she would. Not having had a mother since I was six, I didn't know how good their radar was.

Angie gave me a big hug when she dropped me off. "I'll miss you, kiddo," she said.

"I'll miss you too," I whispered around a sudden lump in my throat.

"Don't be too mad at that boyfriend of yours. Call me anytime."

So I hadn't fooled her, after all. After one last hug, I got out and went in the house, where my dad pretended he hadn't been waiting up for me but had accidentally fallen asleep in front of the TV.

Theo sent me photos from "middle of nowhere Nebraska," some really pretty ones from Wyoming, then from Pocatello,

Idaho, where he texted me: Sorry we had a fight on my last night. I love you—and I texted back that I was sorry too. That was the last I would hear from him until he went into town from camp, whenever that would be.

For the rest of the week, I studied the lessons that were posted online and wrote a paper on ancient Chinese bronze work and hung out with Julia. I also heard from Denny a few times. He said that Frederick was still in the ICU, but things looked good. Denny was starting to get nervous about his next AFF, but he supposed getting cold feet was normal, wasn't it? I wrote back that it was, that everyone gets nervous, that he'd be crazy not to be.

My dad wanted to leave for the DZ on Friday right after I finished an online quiz. He said since Theo was gone, there was no reason for me to stick around at home. "I have other friends too, you know, not just Theo," I pointed out. "I've been studying hard all week and I'm going to be working all weekend. Don't I get Friday evening off? And don't you want to see Elise?" He relented, so I went to a party at my friend Nicole's house. Of course my dad called first to make sure her parents would be there. They were, but they might as well not have been because they always stayed in their room with the door closed when Nicole had people over. They had an amazing game room and didn't seem to be bothered by noise.

When I got to Nicole's, a bunch of people were already there. Music was blaring in the den, and the TV was on with the sound turned off, tuned to a program that showed idiots getting into painful-looking accidents on skateboards.

Nobody paid attention either to the music or to the idiots on the screen.

I got some soda in a red cup and wandered through the den, greeting some people here and there. I'd known most of them since I was little. I blew a kiss to Cory, who had been my boyfriend in sixth grade, and as always, he clapped his hand to his cheek like the kiss had smacked him and pressed his other hand to his heart, pretending to swoon with love. His girlfriend, Hannah, fake-slapped him and then gestured at me to come over.

I wove my way through the crowd, saying hi to people and tripping over feet. When I reached them, Hannah said, "About time you got here! I thought I'd have to listen to him sing along with every song. Can you take a turn minding him while I get a drink?"

"My tunefulness pleaseth you not?" Cory asked.

"Nay, fair sir, your tunefulness pleaseth none," I said. "It is sorely lacking in, er, tune."

After our eighth-grade field trip to see *Macbeth*, for a while everybody in our class had spoken Shakespearean—or what we called "Shake-speech." Cory and I were the only ones who still did it. We could keep it going forever or until we drove everyone around us crazy, which was usually the point.

Hannah had an even lower tolerance for Shake-speech than most of our friends. She stuck her fingers in her ears and said, "La-la-la-la-la" to drown us out.

"Yon wench hath stopped up the access and the passage to her ears," I told Cory, but Hannah heard, because she took out her fingers and said, "Who you calling wench, wench?" before leaving to refill her drink.

"I see not thy paramour," Cory said.

"He hath departed for the wilds of Idaho, where he will instruct the youth of that kingdom in the art of climbing rocks."

"Seriously?" Cory asked, dropping the Shake-speech. "For how long?"

"All summer."

"Good," he said. Cory didn't like Theo—and Theo didn't like Cory—and neither one made a secret of it. "Now's your chance to come to your senses. Maybe when Mr. Pretty Face is gone you'll realize what a—"

"Cut it out," I said, and swigged my soda. "I'll see you later. Hannah's coming back."

I could have stayed; Hannah knew there was nothing to be jealous about. But I wanted to have fun, not listen to Cory ragging on Theo. So I went upstairs to see what was going on.

I moved past some people playing beer pong and went to the card table, which was set up with a Scrabble game. A guy named Brian and a girl a year older than us named Maggie were concentrating on the board. A few people watched them. Scrabble seemed awfully tame, but then Maggie laid down some tiles with a flourish and said, "Double word score!" and instead of calculating points and adding them to some tally, she pointed at Brian.

"What are you doing?" I asked. I swirled my soda.

"Strip Scrabble," Maggie said.

"Want to play?" Brian asked.

"Quit stalling," Maggie said to him. "Two items of clothing. And your watch doesn't count. *Or* your glasses," she added as he reached for his face.

"Since when?"

"Since forever." She tapped a tile on the card table.

"Clancy, you're an impartial judge," Brian appealed to me. "What do you say?"

"Remove thy garments," I said darkly. So off came his shirt and one shoe.

"Care to join us?" he asked.

"I doff my raiment for no one," I said.

"Oh, come on," Maggie said. I had been in junior English with her that year, when I was a sophomore. "You know more words than the rest of us put together."

I hesitated another moment, then sat down and reached into the bag and pulled out seven tiles. Theo would have said something about how stupid the game was, but Theo wasn't there. My dad wasn't there. I wasn't sure whether I was playing because I wanted to or because my dad and Theo would hate it. I told myself I didn't care.

Anyway, Maggie was right about my vocabulary, and I would probably end up with all my clothes still on.

The rules of Strip Scrabble, which seemed to change at every round, were pretty complicated, but it turned out to be fun in a nerdy kind of way. Maggie was hilarious and Brian was pretty bad at Scrabble. Pretty soon he was down to his boxers, and a small crowd had gathered. There were hoots of "Take it off!" and someone hummed "The Stripper."

"Stop it!" Nicole shout-whispered, glaring at her parents' closed door. Evidently there were a few things that would alert them.

It was my turn. I had lost both shoes and a sock but was still decent. I studied my tiles and then added an *s* to "herd" to spell out "sherd."

Silence.

"There's no such word," a girl said.

"She's just faking you out, man," said someone else.

Brian studied my face. I tried to act like I was faking but hoping he'd believe me.

"Why wouldn't she just spell 'herds,' then? She must know 'sherd' is real or she wouldn't risk a challenge."

I tapped my finger on the letter *a*, one square past the end of "sherd," which would have prevented me from putting anything there.

"Oh."

"So challenge her!" Brian said.

Maggie stretched. "Not me, dude. I don't care if it's a real word—I can afford to take something off." She held up a foot and wiggled her toes in her sandals. "You can't."

He chewed on his lip. Finally, he said, "I challenge you." He typed a few letters on the iPad on the table. When he said, "Oh crap," everyone shrieked with laughter.

"So what does it mean?" somebody asked.

"'Sherd,'" Brian read. "'Variant of shard. A fragment, usually of pottery.'"

"Remove thy garment posthaste," I said.

A girl chanted, "Take it off, take it off, take it *off*," until

Nicole's mom came out of her room. She acted like she was getting some popcorn, but it was enough to end the game. Brian's look of relief made everyone crack up again. I laughed so hard I felt like I was going to pass out.

I went back downstairs as other people sat down at the Scrabble board and Brian pulled his clothes back on. In the den, Amity, a girl who'd been in my Spanish class, waved me over from the couch, where she was sitting with a cup that I knew probably held beer. Amity was stunning—not cute and round and sexy like Julia, but tall and lean, with straight black hair, amazing green eyes, and features that looked like they were carved from marble. "Protect me," she muttered behind her hand as I sat down.

"From what?"

She darted her eyes to the corner, where a bunch of guys stood laughing in the way that means they know you're looking at them. "Which one?" I asked, and she gave me a look. "Oh, I see. All of them."

She groaned and leaned back on the sofa cushions. Her long legs looked even longer in her skintight jeans and high-heeled suede boots. Anyone else would have been uncomfortably hot in the Missouri June, but Amity didn't have a drop of sweat on her. "My mom almost didn't let me come," she confided. "She said all teenage boys are only after one thing, and she didn't trust them around me." She laughed, a surprisingly throaty laugh. "She should know!" Everyone knew that her mom was just sixteen years older than she was and looked like she was Amity's big sister. The boys went glassy-eyed at the sight of her whenever she came to our school.

"So what changed her mind?" I asked Amity. "Your mom, I mean, about you coming to the party?"

"You did."

"Me?"

"I told her you'd be here and she said, 'That's okay, then.'"

"So I'm like a chaperone?"

I tried not to sound pissy, but Amity said, "Oh no, it's not like that at all. Just that you're, you know, you don't . . ." She trailed off.

Then something changed. I couldn't quite define it; it was like when you stare at one of those drawings that look like a candlestick, and all of a sudden you see that it's also two profiles facing each other. What changed was how I saw myself, my life, Theo, my dad, and it was so obvious that I didn't think I could ever see it the other way again, like when the image flips back and forth between the candlestick and the profiles. Something wasn't the way it appeared.

I was still thinking of myself the way my dad saw me—unable to make quick decisions, fragile—but my friends thought of me as solid, sensible, kind of prudish. *Which one was I? The two faces or the candlestick? Or neither one?*

I was tired of the way people made up their minds about me. And I was also tired of being too scared of making my dad go through another loss to even take a little risk. It was getting ridiculous. I couldn't play it safe my whole life, or even just until I went off to college.

Only, I didn't know how to take risks. I wasn't stupid—I wasn't about to play Russian roulette or shoot up drugs or steal a car. Still, I felt like I was going to suffocate if I

123

didn't do something, anything, that nobody expected of me. *But what?*

Amity looked uncomfortable, and I realized that I was staring at her. The party feeling had fled, and I stood up. "I've got to go. Have to get up early in the morning." I couldn't stay at the party if I was there as some kind of chaperone. Plus, I wanted to get back to the quiet of my room so I could think.

"But you just got here," Amity said, and I told her I had only wanted to stop by and say hi to some people, and I'd already been there longer than I'd planned.

I called my dad and said I didn't feel well, and then went outside. He pulled up a few minutes later. He frowned at the lights and the noise and the number of people spilling out onto the sidewalk. "You okay?" he asked as I climbed in.

"Bellyache." If he assumed I was talking about cramps, he'd never ask a follow-up question, and sure enough, he didn't say anything. Or maybe he thought I had left because the party was too wild, and he didn't want to spook me out of this proper behavior by praising me for it.

As we got out of the car at home, I said, "Let's spend tomorrow night at the DZ, okay? There's nothing going on here and Theo's gone, and I can get more studying done where there aren't distractions."

"You sure?" He sounded tentative but pleased.

I nodded.

"You don't want to go out with Julia tomorrow night?"

I shook my head. "She'll be doing something with Justin. It's their first-date anniversary."

"Those two are too serious," he said, as I knew he would.

"So you want to spend tomorrow night at the DZ?" I repeated.

"Sure. I'll call Cynthia and ask her to air out the trailer."

When we got home, I closed my bedroom door behind me and exhaled a long breath. As I got ready for bed, I tried to put into words the feeling of recognition I'd had when Amity had said that about me being . . . what? She hadn't finished her sentence, but my mind supplied all sorts of adjectives. *Just that you're reliable. Just that you're trustworthy. You're sensible, mature, responsible, levelheaded.* "Why didn't my parents name me Prudence and get it over with?" I asked out loud.

Only, how could I know if I really was all those things, or if the only reason I behaved reliably, sensibly, maturely, responsibly, prudently was because I was afraid of what would happen if I didn't? Which was the real picture—the candlestick or the profiles? And who was I protecting—my dad or myself?

To go in: To die as a result of impact with the ground. Synonyms: to bounce, to hammer, to crater, to frap (from the French *frapper*, meaning to strike or hit).

—*The Whuffo's Guide to Skydiving*

On Saturday we got to the DZ at dawn, long before there was any work for me to do. I stumbled into the lounge and fell asleep on the brown couch that had replaced the gold-and-green one I had been napping on that day ten years ago.

Ripstop jumped on top of me and curled up on my hip, which was rare—he wasn't usually a cuddler. I half woke when a group came into the office and filled out their forms and made the usual nervous jokes about life-insurance policies and wills, loud enough that I could hear them through the closed door. When Cynthia called the first student load, I woke up for real and sat up, disturbing Rippy, who jumped down and stood at the door, his tail waving. I let him out and followed him into the office.

Cynthia looked up. "Ready for another exciting day at the drop zone?"

I shrugged. Packing rigs got boring, but at least here I wouldn't be reminded of Theo. He had come out to the DZ only once. Good weather for skydiving is the same as good weather for rock climbing, but one time when he'd hurt his shoulder he came to Knoxton with me. He was bored the whole time. Noel entertained himself by telling Theo one shoulda-died story after another—I suspected that not all of them were true—and then some stories about a DZ in the desert where you could take a crater tour.

"Why are there craters at a drop zone?" Theo had asked, which was a mistake.

"Each one was made by a jumper who didn't pull." Noel laughed when comprehension dawned on Theo's face.

"I don't think that's funny," Theo had said stiffly. "And I don't think you should tell those stories in front of Clancy."

Noel looked at me. "You okay with crater stories, Clancy?"

He knew I was. Skydivers are fine with reminders of what skydiving's about. If they weren't, they wouldn't last long at the DZ, because one of the ways jumpers get rid of tension is by sometimes joking about death and sometimes acting like the possibility of it doesn't exist. One of the regular jumpers at Knoxton always used the canopy that his brother had been flying when he went in. Another one had a paper address book so that when someone he knew died, he could stamp over their name with a skull and crossbones. Everyone had different ways to cope.

I flaked the canopy and smoothed it out. "Doesn't bother me. If it did, I'd tell you to shut up." Crater stories and shoulda-died stories *were* fine with me, as long as nobody talked about my mom's accident or about main-reserve entanglements. Everyone at our DZ knew better than to do that.

"Attagirl." Noel gave me a big smacking kiss on the lips and walked out, laughing again.

Theo glared after him. "Is that the gay one or the straight one?"

"The gay one," I had said, lying to keep the peace. When we got home Theo told me he hated the DZ and that he thought jumpers were buffoons ("Except for your dad, of course, and Cynthia seems nice") and that he'd never go back. When Theo says "never" he means "never," and I knew I wouldn't be seeing him at the DZ again. I suspected that there was another reason too—this was a place where nobody except my dad treated me like a fragile little thing, and he would look silly if he tried to be my protector there.

I cranked up my iPod and was setting up the packing table when the guys who had done the seventieth-birthday jump the week before came in. Two of them wore old-style jumpsuits made of heavy cloth, like canvas, in different eighties colors. One was lime green, I swear, and the other was neon orange and black. The loose legs flapped as the guys walked. The other two looked more normal in their jeans and T-shirts. I must have had a grin on my face because the guy wearing lime green said, "What's so funny?" but in a joking way, like he knew how ridiculous they looked.

"Just admiring the ways of the ancestors," I answered.

"You would be wise to learn from those who have gone before, Grasshopper," said a guy with a big gray mustache, also straight out of the eighties. He'd been staring at me earlier, and he smiled now.

"Does your team have a name?" I asked.

"We're not really a team," said the guy in the green jumpsuit.

"Why?" asked the one with the mustache. "Have a suggestion?"

I thought for a moment. I said, "The Geezers?" They laughed, and the first guy said he'd ask his wife to sew a big G on his pack.

A skinny man from their group had spread out his rig on the floor and was staring at it. "Remember how to do it?" I asked. I stopped myself right before finishing with "Grandpa." I realized that he might not find that funny.

He looked up. "You a rigger?"

So someone else thought I looked eighteen.

"Packer. But I can get my dad, or see if one of the other riggers is around if you need some help," I offered.

"Nope." He started to squat, evidently thought better of it, and plopped down on the concrete floor with a grunt. "I'll just . . ." I watched him out of the corner of my eye. He was sloppy, but his pack job was fine.

"Hey!" Denny was in the doorway, already rigged up. Even with the sun at his back, his eyes sparkled with excitement.

"Hey, Denny. Third jump today?"

He nodded. "Just Louisa is going out with me this time."

"Cool." I nodded at the Geezers, who were talking about the good old days again. "You on their load?"

"I think so. Cynthia said it wouldn't be long before she called it. Why don't you come up with us? Would your dad let you?"

"Go for an observer ride? Sure."

"He doesn't worry about you when you go along for the ride?"

I shook my head. "Norton's been flying me around since I was a baby, and my dad knows I'm safer in an aircraft with him than in a car with most people. Skydivers don't think of small planes as anything particularly dangerous."

Denny looked like he didn't believe me.

"You'll just have to take my word for it. My dad's all about the odds. Norton flew in combat, so he can obviously handle Missouri."

"So how about it? Want to come along?"

I hadn't gone up in a long time, and I realized that I had missed looking out the open door at the clouds and the sky. I could use a break anyway, and the Geezers would pack their own rigs, so the only one I'd have to pack when we landed would be Denny's. And it was such a beautiful day. "Let me ask."

Cynthia said the second group of students hadn't arrived yet, so even with the Geezers and Denny's videographer, there'd be room for me.

"Denny's getting this jump filmed too?" I was surprised;

the AFF series already cost more than a thousand dollars and each video would be over a hundred. His parents must really have a lot of money.

"He wants a videographer on each jump," she said. Nice work for whoever was filming it. So in the hangar I put on a rig I had packed. I tightened the straps until they were good and secure.

Denny gave me a quizzical look when I came out. "Why are you wearing a parachute? Are you going to jump?"

"Anyone riding in a plane with an open door has to wear a rig, even the pilot. I would wear one anyway, even if it wasn't a rule."

"So what would you do if you had to jump? Do you know how to land and everything?"

"Kind of." When I was little I'd practiced PLFs by jumping off the packing table. I'd gotten so bruised that a whuffo almost called Child Protective Services, until he saw me doing it himself. I shrugged the pack into a more comfortable position. "If I freak out and don't open on my own, there's an automatic activation device. Plus, the canopy's a reserve, which opens really fast. I might land wrong and break my ankle or something, but that's better than going down with the plane if something bad happens, or falling out the door."

"Makes sense." He jiggled up and down on his toes, and I wondered if he was more nervous or excited.

Since the Geezers were going out first, they were waiting for us to get in the back of the Caravan so they wouldn't have to climb over us to get out. It was a perfect day, almost dead still and with just a few clouds.

Even after my haircut, the wind from the turning propeller blew my hair across my face as I followed Denny up the steps into the plane. I pulled my hair back and tucked as much of it into the neck of my shirt as I could after I settled on the bench next to Denny.

"Oh, don't do that!" The Geezer with the big gray eighties mustache had climbed in and sat down on my other side. "You look just like Jenna with your hair down."

"You knew my mom?" I finally squeaked. So that was why he'd been staring at me earlier.

"Put her out on her first jump. Static line. That was in California. She wasn't much older than you, and you look a lot like her. She was shorter, though."

I already knew I was taller than my mom; everyone said I got my height from my dad. I wished I could ask the Geezer about her, but it was so noisy with the door open that we had to shout, and it felt weird to ask questions about her at the top of my lungs. So I smiled at him, thinking that would have to be the end of it, at least for now, but he leaned in and looked me in the eyes.

"She was one in a million, your mother." He spoke just loud enough for me to hear him. "She looked like a model but could cuss as good as any jumper. She was crazy brave too. Her first jump off static line was out the back of a Skyvan—you know what that is?" I did, but I shook my head so he'd keep talking. "It's a cargo plane that has a huge open back. When I told her to go, she took off running and hollering, and leaped out like one of those cliff divers. She was only eighteen. Every man on the DZ was in love with her."

Tears spilled out of my eyes as I tried to smile at him. He squeezed my hand and then tactfully turned away to adjust a chest strap that didn't need adjusting. Someone closed the door of the Caravan, and the noise level dropped. We took off, and I stared out the window and watched the hangar, the other planes, the trailer, and everything else get small. The small, fluffy clouds below us looked solid, like I could step out of the open door and onto one and bounce on it like a big mattress.

Norton took us to altitude pretty fast, and two of the Geezers climbed out the door and clung to the outside of the plane, the legs of their jumpsuits flapping. The other two joined them inside the doorway and they chorused, "One, two, three" and bombed out, the four of them falling together. I leaned out the door and watched them form a flake and then a star, and then I couldn't see them anymore as we droned on. *Not bad for old guys.*

Denny and Louisa were right behind them, Louisa holding on tight to Denny's rig so they'd be snug up against each other in freefall. Denny looked back at me and gave me a thumbs-up and a grin, and then they were gone. I lay on my belly and watched through the door as they fell beautifully flat and stable. Denny did his practice pull just right, and Louisa made an "okay" sign. She started to track away, and I lost sight of them. Denny would pull as soon as Louisa was clear. I wondered if he savored those few seconds alone or if he couldn't wait to get a canopy over him.

Norton's voice came over the loudspeaker. "Now that it's just us, want to have some fun?"

I gave him a thumbs-up, and he started playing, heading for clouds and yelling, "Bam!" as soon as we entered them, following holes in the clouds until they petered out. It was like a roller-coaster ride. I wondered what it felt like to be in freefall and not in a plane when you hit a cloud. You aren't supposed to jump into clouds because you lose sight of the ground, but some people don't follow those rules very carefully. Anyway, in Missouri clouds can roll in really fast even if you're trying to avoid them. Everyone said that falling through a cloud was like being in heavy fog. Once, Randy had talked about entering one when it started to rain. He was descending at the same speed as the raindrops, and even Randy sounded poetic as he described feeling as though he had stopped falling and was surrounded by little dancing globes.

My mom was still alive when my dad bought the Caravan. We all drove to Little Rock—my parents in the front seat, me and Norton in the back. It was the first time I'd ridden in a car without being in a car seat, and the seat belt seemed flimsy. I felt like I was going to slide off onto the floor. Norton didn't say anything to me, but while he and my dad told stories about their days in Iraq until my mom begged them to stop, he held my hand in a firm grip that told me I was okay. He didn't let go until we got to the small airport where the Caravan was waiting.

After Norton had inspected the plane and my dad had paid the owner, Norton climbed in to fly it home to Missouri. I pitched such a fit about driving back without him that my dad signaled him to stop, and he lifted me up and put me in the plane. We got back to the Knoxton DZ about two hours before my parents, and by the time they arrived, I was so stuffed with candy and soda that I threw up on the way home. Norton still teases me about it sometimes.

We landed. "Thanks!" I called to Norton as I climbed down. I stood aside as the students got in, resisting the urge to say, "Whomp!" I didn't know whether it was watching the jumps or Norton's joyride at the end that had left me feeling so up.

I shrugged my rig off. The hangar was empty except for Ripstop. I scooped him up and kissed the side of his face while he squirmed and finally nipped my nose. I dropped him and he bounced out, holding his tail high in indignation.

Voices drifted in from the landing area, and when I looked out I saw that Denny had landed. From the way he was being high-fived, I guessed he had nailed the landing. Soon he came in and undid his straps. He handed the rig to me.

"How was it?"

"Awe-*some*." He split up the two syllables for emphasis. "It really was. I can't wait to go out alone."

"Aren't you even a little scared?"

"I'm a lot scared. But knowing the awesomeness is coming is bigger than the fear. And I guess the fear is even part of the awesomeness, you know?"

"Well, no, I don't."

"Trust me."

I tossed his rig on the table and spread out the canopy,

smoothing the fabric methodically. It was like a tranquilizer, the familiar repeated motions of flaking the cells, pulling the slider up, and then folding, straightening out, and stowing the lines. It kept me from having to answer Denny too.

When I looked up he was watching me. "Going up again later?" I asked.

"If there's time. There are a lot of students ahead of me. You going for another observer ride?"

I shook my head. "I hardly ever do. Only when the plane isn't full, so I'm not taking the place of a paying customer." I closed the pack, making sure it was all nice and tight. I hung it on the wall and turned to see Denny still there. He looked like he wanted to say something.

"What?" I asked, even though I could guess what he was going to say, and sure enough, he asked, "So really—why is it you don't jump?"

I looked at him as I chewed the inside of my cheek. I started to speak, stopped, and then blurted, "Did you google the accident, the one I told you about that happened here ten years ago?" My breath came fast and my face turned hot. I'd told myself that I wanted to be the one to tell someone, and Denny was becoming important to me—no, it was just that he was so easy to talk to. That's why I was saying this, I told myself. But it was harder than I'd thought.

He looked embarrassed. "Sure. Wouldn't you?"

"Did you see the name of the person in the accident?"

"No, I just skimmed it. Didn't want to freak myself out of jumping again."

"So you didn't see that she was married to the owner of

the drop zone? And that her name was Jenna Clancy?" I waited, my heart pounding, while he looked puzzled.

Comprehension dawned. "Shit—that was your mother?"

I nodded. "She—" I cleared my throat.

Denny just looked at me, not urging me to speak, not telling me I didn't have to say anything, neutral. I almost said I didn't want to talk about it, but then the words came tumbling out of my mouth. "It's because of my mom that I—well, really, I don't know how I feel about it. She loved it, so maybe I would too. But it killed her, and maybe it would kill me too. Anyway, my dad doesn't want me to. After my mom went in—" My throat closed, and I looked at him bleakly.

"Oh shit, Clancy." More silence. Then, "Were you there?"

I nodded and took a deep breath. I'd never had to tell anybody what had happened, not really, except Dr. Mike. "I wasn't feeling well, and I was crying for my mom to take me home. She said she had to make one more jump with her team before a meet the next weekend. I knew how important meets were, but I was coming down with the flu, even though nobody knew it yet, and I kept whining until she finally said, 'Just one more, Carys, and that will be all. Just one more jump.' Of course, she meant one more jump that day, but as it turned out . . . Anyway, she tried to kiss me and I wouldn't let her, so she left and I never saw her again."

"Did you see it happen?" His voice was soft, and I liked that he didn't tell me that it didn't matter, that I was a sick little kid, that he was sure my mom knew I loved her, the way Dr. Mike had said. I already knew all that, and it didn't make me feel better.

"I was inside," I said. "In the lounge, you know, that room behind the office?" I could still picture it, the way it had looked then, with the old gold-and-green Goodwill couch, the TV where I watched fuzzy cartoons, my dad's skydiving trophies on a low table, and the nasty indoor-outdoor carpeting with stains from coffee and who knew what else all over it.

I realized I was staring into space.

"Isn't it sad for you to spend every weekend here, where it happened?" Denny asked.

I shook my head. "I like being at the DZ. My mom was so happy here—she wasn't the kind of mom who had fun shopping or hanging out with her girlfriends or anything. She never even really seemed like herself when we were home. I mean, I know she liked being with me, but I could tell that when she did regular mom stuff with me, like playing dress-up and decorating cupcakes, she was pretty bored. When we were here . . ." I let my voice trail off, remembering how her face lit up and her voice got louder whenever we were at the DZ. One night there was a bonfire with music. I sat on my mom's lap, and when she laughed at the stories, I bounced up and down. That was the weekend before she died.

Denny looked unconvinced.

"Anyway, it's not like that for jumpers. I don't think of the DZ as a place of death or anything. Like, if your mom died in your house, it probably wouldn't make you never want to go home again, right? Because it's also where you had Christmas—"

"Hanukkah."

"And played with your cat—"

"Dog."

"Denny!" He made me laugh with frustration, which was probably his intention. "You know what I'm saying. I played with Barbies on this same packing table. And once, on the Fourth of July, Norton flew us from here to the city, where we saw the fireworks from above, which was as awesome as it sounds, and I used to do my homework on Cynthia's computer. When I was really little, I played "manifest" and booked jumps on my toy phone. And we came right back out here after my mom's funeral. My dad couldn't afford not to. So it seems like a natural place to hang out. Plus, like I said, I didn't actually see my mother go in."

"That's good. God, that sounds stupid."

"No, you're right, it *is* good. But my dad saw it, and I couldn't do that to him—have him see it twice. So that's why I don't know if I'll ever make a jump."

That wasn't the only reason, though. I didn't know how to explain to Denny, without being melodramatic about it, that the same thing that scared the pants off me also drew me to it, like a horror-movie monster that makes the heroine follow it into a trap, even though the whole audience is shouting at her not to do it.

FACT: There have always been female skydivers. The first woman known to make a successful parachute jump from an airplane and the first person in the world to make an intentional freefall jump was five-foot-tall, eighty-five-pound Georgia "Tiny" Broadwick in 1913.

—*The Whuffo's Guide to Skydiving*

I tossed a rig onto the table and straightened the lines while I waited for Denny to say something about my mother having a six-year-old daughter ten years ago, making me only sixteen. He didn't. Either he had really only skimmed the article, like he'd said, or he hadn't noticed that, or he thought that the reporter had gotten it wrong.

Cynthia called a load. "That's me!" Denny said.

"Have fun," I said automatically.

"I'll do my best," he answered, and then he was out the door.

My phone rang. Theo, finally! I walked outside. "Hello?"

"Hi, sweetheart," Theo said. I loved when he called me that; it was so old-fashioned and romantic.

"Where are you calling from?"

"I had to come into town to pick up a climbing rope. I don't have much time to talk, but I wanted to tell you I miss you and that the camp posted some pictures on their website. I think I'm in some of them."

"How is it?"

He went on for a while about how great the camp was and how beautiful Idaho was and how much he liked the other counselors. He said that most of the kids were great too, except for a few who were homesick and one who ignored the safety briefings, so they were going to have to scare her for her own good. I wondered whether he was ever going to ask how I was doing.

He finally slowed down and asked after my dad. "Fine," I said. "He's been seeing more of that Elise woman, I think."

"Uh-huh."

I could tell he wasn't paying attention. "Theo, you there?"

"Yeah, right here. How's your summer going?"

I should've probably said something about Denny, but somehow I didn't want to. "Good. My dad's paying me by the hour now instead of by the pack job, and I'm running some errands in the car. And Angie was here, but she's gone back to New Mexico. Jackson did a tandem a little while ago."

He didn't answer, and once again I said, "You there? Theo?" Why couldn't he focus on our conversation?

Then he was back. "Sorry—someone asked me a question."

"Where are you? I thought you were in some sport-supply place getting rope or whatever."

"Some of the other counselors came too," he added, and then obviously not to me he said, "Just a sec." Then he came back. "Sorry, Clancy, I have to deal with this."

"Thanks for calling. I'll check out those photos," I said.

"I miss you."

"Miss you too. I love you."

"Love you too. Bye."

Then he was gone. I glanced in the hangar but Denny hadn't come back yet. I sighed. Great. After the way Theo had acted all distracted and busy, I almost wished I had ignored my phone and kept talking with Denny. He was going to be a good shrink one day. He was making me think about things I was happier avoiding but that I should probably have been thinking about.

Enough about Denny, I scolded myself.

The PA crackled, and Cynthia's voice said, "Clancy to the office."

Good. Something to do. When I got there, Cynthia stood up stiffly and stretched. "You got a few minutes to mind the phones for me?" she asked. "There's room on the next load and if I don't do a jump soon I'm going to lose my mind."

"Heaven forfend," I said as I took her seat and she grabbed her rig off the hook behind the door.

The phone rang a lot while she was gone. I set up a tandem jump for the next weekend with a nervous whuffo

142

who wanted a lot of details and statistics about safety. I had worked the phones and even the manifest a lot of times, and I understood Cynthia's abbreviations and special notes, so I entered the information on her spreadsheet.

Scheduling jump students is more complicated than it looks, partly because fun jumpers usually show up without making appointments. If they don't get to jump at Knoxton, they're likely to take their business over to the Jump Ranch, even if it does have kind of a shady reputation. So my dad has to make sure there are enough pilots to fly the students, plus at least one more for the fun jumpers. But if the students don't show up—students chicken out all the time—and my dad has arranged for more pilots and planes, he still has to pay the pilots, even if they don't fly.

So Cynthia had to keep an eye on numbers, and when it looked like things were going to be really busy, my dad would hire someone with a Twin Otter or a King Air or another jump plane. Once, a DC-3 was going across the country, stopping at DZs here and there, and it stayed at Knoxton for two weeks. So many people came that even Raymond, the owner of the Jump Ranch, finally gave up and closed down for the weekend. He came out himself and made some jumps. I'd heard so many bad things about the Jump Ranch that I was surprised when he seemed like a regular jumper and not some evil being.

When the phone finally fell silent, I thought I should look at Theo's camp photos. That would make me miss him and stop feeling annoyed with him.

The landscape in Idaho was totally different from that

of Missouri, with mountains and cliffs, and even the trees looked different. Darker, I guessed. The camp itself looked pretty standard, with log cabins clustered around a flagpole, and there were lots of pictures of kids mugging for the camera and paddling canoes.

There was a photo of two people climbing a cliff face, taken from way below. I recognized Theo instantly; he always looked like a spider when he climbed, with his long arms and legs reaching holds that no one else could get to. The other climber was a girl. The next shot was of them at the top of the cliff, arms around each other, smiling and holding their fists in the air in triumph. I leaned closer to the screen. The girl's name was Ali, according to the caption, and she was cute—short, with a brown ponytail and freckles. She looked athletic and muscular, and she had a wide grin.

It was about time for Cynthia's jump, so I closed the site and put the phone on voice mail, and stepped outside with the binoculars. She was always fun to watch.

Cynthia had gone to college on an acrobatics scholarship and did amazing things in freefall. As I watched, she went head-down and rotated like a propeller, and then did some backflips and some other moves that I couldn't imagine doing on a mat in a gym, much less while falling through the sky.

She stood up the landing, took off her rig, and did a cartwheel. The students watching burst into applause and she bowed with a flourish. I went back inside and checked the voice mails while Cynthia packed her rig. When she came back I said, "Amazing!"

"Thanks." She slung her rig on its hook.

Even though Cynthia's jump had been awesome, it wasn't enough to distract me from the picture of Theo. *Why was he hugging that girl? Okay, maybe they were celebrating a hard climb or something, but the way she was leaning into him and he was squeezing her looked . . . too cozy somehow.* I told myself to quit being paranoid.

A commotion arose out in the landing area: someone calling my dad, loud voices, running feet. Cynthia and I looked at each other, frozen for an instant. The sound meant only one thing: a jumper was in trouble.

Cynthia and I ran out together, ignoring the ringing phone. My dad stood in the field next to Noel, shading his eyes from the sun and talking into the headset. I couldn't hear what he was saying, but he sounded firm and calm. Louisa and Randy were standing next to each other, holding their bunched-up canopies. Other people looked up, pointing and speaking in low tones. The sky held only one jumper under canopy. At first I didn't see anything wrong, but then I realized that for some reason the jumper wasn't turning to face into the wind. It had to be a student.

He was going pretty fast. At this rate, whoever it was would wind up in the next county—if he was lucky. There were a lot of power lines in the direction he was heading, and that could mean big trouble. Parachutes are really steerable, but students don't usually have the hang of it.

"He opened just fine," Randy was saying. "We tracked away, and when I was open I looked back, and everything looked okay."

"Nobody's blaming you." Noel sounded grim.

Oh no, please not Denny, I thought, but there was Denny on the edge of the field, squinting up at the sun like everyone else.

I went over to Louisa. "Who is it?"

"That college kid who did an AFF a week ago." She sounded tense.

"Travis?" *Oh no.*

She nodded. "He was totally freaked out last weekend, but he came back during the week and did the rest of the course."

What was he doing? Proving something to the girl who Randy had been flirting with? Of all the bad reasons to skydive, proving something to someone else is about the worst.

"This is his second solo," Louisa said. "He did fine the first time. I probably should have run through steering once more, but he seemed okay, and honestly, how hard is it to steer?"

When Denny glanced in my direction, I waved at him. He trotted over and shrugged off his harness. "What's going on? Where's he going?"

"He's supposed to be heading this way." I looked at the wind sock. "I don't know why he isn't."

My dad said into the microphone, "It's normal to drop a little when you turn. You're tucking in an edge of the parachute when you pull down on the toggle, so of course there's less of it holding you up, and you'll descend a bit faster. It'll go back to normal as soon as you release the toggle."

The student must have answered, because my dad said, "No, you're just fine. You're nowhere near the ground, and you have lots of room to play with. Now let me see you pull on the right toggle a little. Come on . . ." He looked at Cynthia.

"Travis," she supplied.

"Come on, Travis. Let's see a little turn." After an agonizing moment, the right-hand edge of the canopy bent down a bit. Travis let go of the turn almost right away. He must have screeched, because my dad winced and pulled the headset away from his ears.

"That was great." He settled the headset back down. "Do it again, and hold it down a little farther and for a little longer. You're still heading downwind, and unless you turn into the wind, you'll have a rough landing."

He turned the microphone away from his mouth and said, "Randy, go out and ride along the road west of Knoxton. He'll come down out there someplace."

Randy started unbuckling his harness, but before he could finish I ducked back into the office and grabbed my dad's car keys off the hook. I ran to the lot and started the car. My dad was talking to Travis and didn't even turn around. My heart was pounding, and it wasn't just because I was afraid that something would happen to Travis. I felt guilty that I had talked him into jumping when he was so scared. Maybe if I hadn't convinced him, he wouldn't have jumped last weekend and he'd have quit. Or he might have waited until he was in a better frame of mind.

I tossed my phone onto the dashboard and adjusted the seat. The passenger door opened and Denny hopped in. "Would it help if I watch where he's going while you drive?" he asked.

"Sure. Call my dad and tell him we're going to get him. It would take Randy too long to get his rig off and everything." I gave him the number as I pulled out of the lot. Denny relayed the message and I turned onto the road.

If Travis hit the power lines, it would make no difference when we got there because he would have already sizzled. If he didn't hit them and he did an okay landing, the worst that could happen would be landing in a cow pie. But if he was freaked out, he might botch the landing and break something. Or worse.

I had to slow for an Amish wagon. I gripped the steering wheel, muttering, "Come on, come on," and as soon as the road widened, I zoomed around it. "Do you see him?" I asked Denny.

"Pretty much straight ahead. Heading left."

"This road curves right soon," I said. "I think if I turn left at the next—" My phone rang. "Could you get that? It might be my dad. They can see him from a different angle."

It was Cynthia. After conferring with her, Denny said, "She says it looks like he'll come down near the farm with the vegetable stand. You know the one she means?"

I nodded as I tore into the left-hand turn, scattering gravel. "We're heading for it now. Do you still see him?"

"Yep. He's getting awfully low."

"Facing into the wind?"

There was a pause while Denny looked at the trees to see which way the leaves were blowing. "I don't think so."

The kind of canopy Travis was flying has a forward drive of about fifteen miles per hour. So if there's a wind of, say, ten miles per hour, that means a jumper heading downwind will be going forward at twenty-five, which would mean a really hard landing. But if he faces into the wind, he'll be going only five miles per hour. That's why it's important to be turned the right way.

We were pretty far away, and it looked like Travis was going to come down on the other side of a small hill. I didn't know if my dad could see him anymore. That meant my dad couldn't talk him through the landing, and since Travis was so wired, he'd probably flare way high and come crashing down. I sped up.

The road curved around the little hill, and I caught a glimpse of the green-and-white canopy, and then I saw Travis. He was holding the steering toggles but not pulling down on them. The power lines stretched across the road, marked by what looked like basketballs.

"Ruh-roh." Denny glanced at me.

"Call my dad, quick, and tell him to tell Travis to pull his feet up." He did, and Travis bent his knees as he went over the road. I don't know if he would have brushed against the power lines if he hadn't, but it would have been close.

The road dipped around the hill, and I lost sight of him again. Denny muttered, "Come on, come on, come on," although whether he was telling me to go faster or willing Travis to do a good landing, I didn't know.

The road sloped upward, and there was Travis. He was still heading downwind, but luckily the wind had dropped some. I drove as close to the field as I could, slammed on the brakes, and raced out of the car. I yelled, "Flare! Flare *right now!*"

I hoped he could hear me and also that he would manage to do it. And miraculously, he did. He pulled down on the toggles—he was so close now that I could see his lips set in a tight line—and the forward motion of the canopy slowed. He swung forward nice and easy and touched down. Anybody could have stood it up, but he didn't even try, or maybe his knees were wobbly, because he stumbled forward and collapsed. He lay facedown without moving.

Denny came running. At the crest of the next hill was the little farm stand, with a few cars and pickups near it. Some of the cars were heading our way—curious whuffos, probably. I hoped at least one of them was a doctor or nurse or paramedic.

Before we reached Travis, he sat up and leaned forward. He puked on the grass, pressed his hand to his chest, and puked again. Phew. Not seriously hurt if he could sit up by himself. Denny said into the phone, "He seems okay. We'll call you back as soon as we know for sure."

I pulled off Travis's goggles. "You okay?" I asked. "How was the landing? Did you hurt anything?"

"I don't know," Travis confessed. "I was just so glad to be on the ground that I didn't even notice." He started to push himself up to his feet, but I told him to wait a minute and gathered up the canopy. I nodded at Denny and he gave Travis a hand up.

"Nothing hurts," Travis said, leaning to one side and then the other, testing his ankles.

Denny handed me the phone. I told Cynthia, "He's on his feet. He didn't hit too hard, I don't think." We walked to the car, watched by a silent group of whuffos. They were probably disappointed not to see any blood or broken bones.

Now that it was over, I wondered what my dad would say when I got back. I rehearsed my answer: "I have a license, it's a country road in the middle of the day, I drove carefully, Randy would have had to take off his rig to drive, and that would have taken too long . . ."

I don't care, I told myself. *Let him get mad. I did the right thing.*

As I helped Travis settle into the backseat, one of the whuffos said, "I don't see why anyone would jump out of a perfectly good airplane." I knew that Denny was now a for-real jumper because he rolled his eyes and grimaced at me.

I called my dad. "We're on our way back," I told him, and held my breath.

"Tell Denny not to call me again while he's driving," he said. "And take it slow. I want Travis to have some time to process what happened before I talk to him." I was tempted to tell him that I'd been the one driving, but reason prevailed, and all I said was that we'd take our time.

"Why don't you drive, Denny?" I asked. "I'll sit back here with Travis."

"So what happened up there?" Denny asked Travis as we drove off.

I glanced at Travis. He was looking out the window, his hair matted to his head. "I'm not sure. It suddenly all seemed so real, you know? Every time I made a turn, I kind of swung out and it felt like a roller coaster, and I realized how much faster I dropped. It panicked me, and I thought that if I just let go of everything and let it happen, it would all take care of itself somehow." He had the grace to look embarrassed.

"The canopy ride didn't bother you on your first jump?" Denny asked.

Travis shook his head. "I was so full of adrenaline that time that I didn't notice."

I didn't want to embarrass him further, so I asked carefully, "Did they tell you about heading into the wind?"

"Uh-huh."

"And about the power lines out in this direction?"

He didn't answer, and I saw that he was white. I shouldn't have reminded him about how close he had come to frying himself.

"Pull over," I said urgently. Denny did, and I jumped out and yanked the door open just in time for Travis to throw up onto the side of the road. I took a bottle of water out of the trunk. It was warm and so old that it probably tasted like plastic, but I didn't think he'd notice. I gave it to him along with an ancient piece of gum I found in the glove compartment.

Travis lay down in the backseat—I didn't have the heart to make him buckle up—and I sat in the passenger seat, next to Denny.

At the DZ everyone was going about their business again now that the excitement was over. My dad led Travis into the office for a "debriefing," which I knew would end with him telling Travis that he recommended that he stop jumping, at least for now. He wouldn't let him jump at

Skydive Knoxton again without going through another AFF course. I didn't think Travis would ever come back, though. I think he'd had enough of trying to impress that girl.

All of a sudden I burst into tears. I clamped my hand over my mouth to hold in the sobs and ran to the hangar, which was blessedly empty. I buried my face in a musty old canopy and cried and cried.

When I finally stopped I sat up and wiped my eyes, knowing that I was smearing dust and dirt around my face. What the hell had just happened? Why was I crying?

Because if he'd died, it would have been your fault, said the cold little voice inside of me.

I knew it wouldn't have been my fault. But knowing you're not responsible for someone's death and feeling it were two different things. That was something I'd known forever—at least ever since Dr. Mike.

I'd thought, until Angie finally convinced my dad to take me to Dr. Mike, that it was my fault that my mom had died. Even years later, when I knew that the problem had been a bag lock, I thought that if she hadn't been so distracted by my crying, she would have been able to clear it.

I also thought my dad blamed me for her going in. Sometimes I caught him looking at me in a way that made me wonder if he'd overheard me whining that day, or if she'd told him about it. I couldn't ask him and he'd never bring it up, so I'd never know.

And then I'd talked Travis into jumping last weekend, when he was so scared that he probably should have stayed on the ground. That jump had gone okay, which had probably encouraged him to think it would be a cinch the next time. But it looked like his terror ramped up instead of getting better. That happens sometimes. You'd think that if someone jumped and lived, they'd start getting over the fear, but sometimes it gets worse.

Someone came in, and I turned my back to the door so they wouldn't see my tear- and dust-streaked face. I started to pack the rig on the top of the big pile waiting for me, but my hands were trembling. *Adrenaline*, I told myself. *Not guilt? Not a reminder of . . . another accident, perhaps?* that cold little voice asked.

"No," I muttered. "That was totally different." The complete opposite, in fact. I'd tried to talk my mom *out* of jumping that day, not into it, and besides, I wasn't a little kid now. I didn't believe in magical thinking anymore. What I'd said to my mom had nothing to do with what happened then, and what I said to Travis had nothing to do with today.

I took a deep breath, willed my hands to stop shaking, and got to work.

When I went into the office a little later, Cynthia was on the phone with a vendor, not paying any attention to Travis, who was talking to Randy. I lingered a bit to eavesdrop, but Randy's tone was so low that I could catch only a word here and there. He looked devious, or maybe he just looked like Randy. There wasn't much difference.

"—Jump Ranch," I heard Randy say. "They won't check."

Travis murmured something and I could guess what Randy'd been telling him: that if he wanted to jump again, he could always go to the Jump Ranch. As long as he had the logbook showing his AFF jumps, they'd probably figure it was his own business whether he freaked out or not.

Randy glanced at me and said something to Travis, who also looked at me, and then they rose and left. What, did Randy think I was going to tattle on him? Jerk.

Cynthia finished her conversation and asked me to mind the phone. While I sat there I pulled up the website of Theo's camp again. I stared at Theo and the girl—Ali—on top of the mountain. She was grinning straight into the camera, but he was looking down at her with a smile so sweet, it almost broke my heart. It was like he was proud of her and amazed by being with her all at the same time.

Cynthia came back. "Thanks for taking over," she said as I quickly closed the page.

The way Theo was looking at Ali bothered me all the way back to the rear of the hangar, where I told myself that there was some logical explanation, and the next time I talked to Theo I'd find out what it was, and then I'd feel stupid for even worrying about it. It was just because I was still upset about Travis. That's why I was letting myself get all worked up because of a picture of my boyfriend, who loved me, and a girl he hadn't even known this time last week.

I wished there was someone I could talk to. Not Angie, who was worried about Leanne and her grandkids. I'd already unloaded enough on her. Julia would still be at work, and later she'd surely be doing something with Justin.

No, there was only one person I wanted to talk to about this, and she was dead.

13

FACT: Among experienced jumpers, avoidable landing errors—especially flaring too high or initiating a turn too close to the ground—account for a large percentage of skydiving injuries and fatalities.

—*The Whuffo's Guide to Skydiving*

The sun lingered on the horizon. Norton flew a sunset load, which was really pretty because one of the canopies was white and reflected the pink and orange of the sky. The jumpers on that load would pack their own rigs, so I was done for the day. I cleaned up and took my log sheet to the office.

My dad was on the PA system, calling a meeting of all personnel. I started to leave to make dinner (which meant microwaving some boxed mac and cheese, and grilling hot dogs), but just as I reached the door, my dad said, "*All* personnel, C.C. You're on salary now, remember?"

I couldn't very well complain about the policy so soon after my promotion, so I came back in and sat down. Cynthia stayed behind the desk, Leon and Noel sat on the floor, and Randy and Louisa came in and sat on folding chairs, like me. My dad stood in front of Cynthia's desk.

"I don't think I need to tell you," he said, "that what happened today could have been much, much worse. The boy was lucky. He barely missed the power lines, and he came down very close to the road. *We're* also lucky that there weren't a lot of whuffos around. The last thing we need is for someone to post pictures or, God forbid, video of a mess like that online." I winced, thinking of the video of my mom. "We need to reexamine how students are prepared so we can try to prevent this kind of thing from happening again."

"He just freaked out, Dave," Randy broke in. "If someone's going to freak out under canopy, there's no way any amount of training is going to prevent it."

"True," my dad said, "but I'm not really talking about training. I'm saying that the instructors should watch for signs that freaking out is a possibility."

That raised a chorus of "It's *always* a possibility" and "How are you supposed to know that?"

Noel said, "You can never tell. Before Denny did his first AFF, I'd have said that he'd be a screamer all through freefall. You never saw a greener face in your life. But he bombed right out and handled his canopy like a pro, and look how many jumps he's done since then."

Louisa added, "Me too. I thought he was the typical rich

kid who would do one jump and never show up again, but he can't wait to get out the door. So you'd have lost a good AFF student and probably a future jumper if you'd asked us if he was going to freak out."

"I'm just asking you to try to tune in a little more to what they're thinking," my dad said. "Get to know them." I shot a look at Randy and sure enough, he was smirking. If he said something stupid about always being ready to get to know *some* of them—*nudge nudge, wink wink*—my dad would fire him for sure.

"So how can you tell a student who's just the normal amount of nervous from one who's going to fall apart?" Leon asked.

My dad asked, "Any ideas?" Nobody said anything. "Okay, let's think of other students who've had problems and see if we can spot any similarities. Noel, that girl last year who tried to do a hook turn right before landing on her first solo and broke her ankle—she was one of yours, right?"

"Hey," Randy protested. "You're not going to blame Noel for that, are you?"

"Nobody's blaming anyone." Louisa looked at my dad.

Noel said, "She asked a lot about formation. She said she wanted to get off of student status as fast as possible and do the fun stuff, but after her injury, she never came back."

"Who was that?" Randy asked. "I don't remember her."

"Some girl." Noel shrugged. "Mostly jumped during the week. She was a nurse, I think?"

Cynthia tapped on her keyboard. "Ah—here she is. Margaret Finnegan."

The girl whose logbook I had found. I made a mental note to give it to Cynthia after the meeting.

"That's the one," my dad said. "So should her behavior have told us something? Was she reckless, or did she have a hard time following rules? What was it?"

After a while, everyone decided that it was impossible to tell if someone was going to freak out. My dad finally gave up, said something about trying to get to know the AFF students better, and told everyone they could go.

Our trailer was parked behind the office on a kind of unofficial campground with a raggedy volleyball net, two Porta-Johns, and a water spigot. Cynthia and her boyfriend lived in the apartment off the lounge, but anyone else who stayed overnight had to either sleep in the fleabag motel in Knoxton or camp out here. I had loved staying in the trailer when I was little; my mom called it "our little house on the big drop zone." It had seemed so cozy then; now it just felt small and smelled mildewy.

An unfamiliar tent was pitched off to the side as though its owner recognized that they weren't a regular and should be careful not to take up someone's usual spot. The tent was smallish and ragged. It wasn't supposed to rain that weekend, so they'd be okay if they didn't mind mosquitoes.

Headlights swept around as a car pulled into the lot. It must have been the overnighter. I watched as the person parked and got out. Huh. Denny. He saw me looking at him and came over.

"What are you still doing here?" I asked.

"I thought I'd stay the night. No use wasting all that gas going back and forth."

"I didn't think you had to worry about the price of gas." I cringed at my words. "I mean—sorry. I don't know why I said that."

"What do you mean? Why did you think I didn't have to worry about gas?" He sounded perplexed.

"Um, your car, for one thing. I mean, it had to cost a lot, right? And you paid for the whole AFF course up front—"

"I don't have a whole lot of money," he said. "My car was a project. My dad got it for me for my sixteenth birthday from a junkyard for practically nothing, and we spent an entire year making it run and cleaning it up. And someone else is paying for my jumps."

I didn't know how to ask who without seeming nosy. He answered anyway.

"Frederick's parents are paying for the AFF course. And the videos."

"Why?"

"It was something Frederick and I were going to do together—make a jump, I mean. When we graduated from high school. But then he got sick, and if he ever does make a jump, it won't be for a long time. The chemo made his bones really fragile, and nobody knows if they'll ever get stronger."

I said, "That sucks."

"Yeah. It really does. Anyway, Frederick still wanted me to do it, but I didn't have enough time between graduation and the internship. My parents looked into drop zones around here, and yours had a better reputation than the other one."

"The Jump Ranch."

"Right. That one didn't look safe, they said. And your dad doesn't usually do static line, so if I came here it was AFF or tandem, and I didn't like the idea of tandem. It didn't seem like I would be making the jump, just going along for the ride, but Frederick's dad said they wouldn't pay for AFF—not because it was too expensive, but because it sounded more dangerous."

"Lots of people think that."

"But then Frederick watched the video of my tandem over and over, and when I told his parents I really loved doing it, they changed their minds and bought me the AFF course and a videographer so he could see them all. They said he keeps talking about getting better and making a jump with me." He cleared his throat, and I looked away while he rubbed his eyes.

"You're doing another one tomorrow?" I asked. "What will that make—three?"

"Four."

"Great."

"So—does that kind of thing happen often? Like with Travis?"

I shook my head. "Not really. Sometimes."

"It didn't even occur to me how scary that was until afterward," he said. "I mean, it all happened so fast, and you seemed to know exactly what to do."

"Me? I didn't do anything!"

"You knew to get your dad to tell him to pull his feet up, and you told him to flare at exactly the right second. So you saved his life—"

"Oh, I didn't save—"

Denny went on as though he hadn't heard me. "You at least kept him from getting a broken leg. He needs to buy you a bottle of your favorite booze."

I didn't know what to say, but Denny rescued me. "Hey, I went into Knoxton for dinner and all the diners were closed. Where do you eat around here?"

"The diners are only open for lunch. Everyone in Knoxton eats dinner at home. There's a 7-Eleven in town." I considered. All he could get there would be chips and dip, which wouldn't be the best way to get ready to spend the night in a small tent that looked holey and damp. "Can you wait here a second?"

Back in the office, my dad was going over some papers. He was trying to figure out if he could have deduced something about Travis's state of mind from his handwriting, no doubt. I watched him for a minute. The harsh light of his desk lamp threw shadows under his eyes and accentuated the lines around his mouth. It also showed that he had more gray in his hair than I'd noticed before.

I cleared my throat and asked, "Dad, is it okay if Denny eats with us tonight? There's plenty."

He didn't look up. "Who?" He sounded distant.

"Denny—you know, the AFF student. He's camping out and didn't know that Knoxton closes up at seven o'clock."

He lowered the papers. "You want him to eat with us?"

I explained again. He looked at me over his reading glasses. "Sure. I guess so. You two go ahead. Just leave me something." I lingered. "You want something else?" he asked.

"Nope." I left. It would have been nice if he'd said something about how well I'd handled the Travis situation. He'd probably been too concerned about the DZ's reputation for it to cross his mind. Which was good, I guessed, or he might start wondering why Denny had taken my dad's car and not his own, which might lead him to think that maybe I was the one who'd driven out there. *It's not like this was the first time a student had gotten into trouble*, I told myself. *He's used to having it dealt with. No big deal.*

So a few minutes later Denny was setting up the grill outside the trailer while I boiled water. He made the hot dogs, I made the mac and cheese, and we both drank Cokes. I offered him ice, which he accepted.

"No accounting for taste." I sipped my iceless but perfectly cold drink.

"Why don't you like ice?"

"Kills the bubbles." That's what my mom always said, anyway. Personally, I couldn't tell the difference in the level of carbonation *avec* ice or *sans* ice, but I had started asking for Coke with no ice as soon as I was old enough to order for myself.

My dad's food was getting cold, so I piled it on a paper plate and took it to the office. He grunted his thanks but barely looked up. I tried not to worry about how hard he was working. He had a lot to deal with, what with his business and being a single father—an older father, on top of that.

He'd been almost forty when my mom died. Dealing with me growing up had to be hard, even with Angie to give him advice about my clothes and hair and puberty.

I left his dinner within reach and went back to where Denny was sitting on a camp chair, gazing up at the stars. A little breeze blew just enough to keep the mosquitoes at bay, and I settled on the other chair.

He stretched and yawned. "Sorry. It's just that this is so relaxing. No pressure. At least not until tomorrow morning."

"What kind of pressure are you expecting tomorrow morning? Do you feel like you have to jump because Frederick's parents have already paid for it?"

"Oh no, not at all. They'd be cool if I didn't. But I still get anxiety before the jump, you know? And I always think maybe I've been lucky so far, and I should quit while I'm ahead."

"Jumping is a lot safer than—"

"Yeah, I know. Safer than downhill skiing and riding motorcycles and a lot of other things that people think are okay, and then they say you're crazy for jumping. Like my mom. She wants me to stop, so I didn't tell her I'd be here this weekend."

"Huh. Like my dad. He thinks it's perfectly fine for other people but not for me."

"My mom hitchhiked through Tibet when she was in college, and later she lived in a cottage on a beach in Greece with some guy she hardly knew. She'd die if I ever did anything like that. There should be a name for it—parents who don't want their kids to do things that they did themselves and survived."

"So come up with a name, Mr. Psychologist."

He frowned in thought for a minute. "I know—the Icarus Complex."

"The what?" I asked.

"Remember that Greek myth, the one about the father and son who flew out of a tower with wings they made from feathers and wax?"

Every jumper knew that story. "Right. The father told his son not to fly too close to the sun or the wax would melt."

"The son was named Icarus," Denny said. "They both flew out of the tower even though the father didn't think his son could handle it, and it turns out he was right. Icarus got carried away with how much fun it was to fly, and he *did* go too close to the sun. I bet if his dad hadn't told him about it, it wouldn't even have occurred to him."

"And the wax melted, and he fell into the sea and drowned. Typical story about how teenagers are impulsive and won't wear their seat belts."

"Exactly," Denny said. "You know some parent made up that myth to scare their kid. And that was the first example of the Icarus Complex."

We talked for a long time—about his work in the lab (he said they didn't hurt the monkeys, just used them in experiments about sharing and cooperation); about Frederick, who was having graft versus host issues, which meant that his body was trying to reject the bone marrow that had been injected into him; about Randy and the other instructors; about my art history class; about Denver and skiing and snowboarding. Denny asked me why we didn't live in Knoxton, but made that long commute every weekend day.

"We did live here until I was about to start kindergarten, and then my mom said we had to move to Hawkins," I told him. "It supposedly has the best public schools in the county." I didn't tell him that I found out that after she died, my dad was planning to move the two of us back to Knoxton, but Dr. Mike said it would be hard on me to lose my house and my friends and school after losing my mom, so we stayed.

We talked about a lot of things, but one subject that didn't come up was Theo. Somehow, when I talked about what there was to do in Hawkins, I told Denny about Julia and Cory, partying at Nicole's, and going to Manuelito's, and I never mentioned Theo once.

14

After most of the morning fog burned off, the sky was a soft blue, and the grass, still a pale spring green, sparkled with tiny droplets. The haze meant that visibility was a little lower than usual, but it was still plenty clear enough for skydiving.

The Geezers had arrived just after dawn. While they waited for the fog to lift, they told shoulda-died stories. I could tell by the way they paused and glanced at me and cleared their throats and then laughed that they were leaving out some details, probably having to do with jumping under the influence. I wondered if things had changed all over the skydiving world in the decades since these guys were young, or if it was just my dad who was so strict about sober jumping.

What looked like a whole college fraternity showed up next. I recognized them; they'd come a few weeks before, but the wind had risen and they'd had to go home without making their jumps. My dad had told them that the earlier they got there, the calmer it was likely to be. The forecast said winds five to ten, so they'd probably make it out this time. Not all of them looked like they thought this was good news.

It was so busy in the hangar that I didn't have time to take a break, except to run to the Porta-John and handle the phones for Cynthia once or twice. Denny came in after his fourth AFF, his rig bundled in his arms. I glanced up from the packing table. "How'd it go?" I didn't really need to ask; his face was practically glowing, his eyes sparkling even more than usual.

"Great!" I could swear I heard three exclamation points. "Where do you want this?" He held up his bundled-up rig.

"Over there. On top of those others."

He dropped the jumble of lines and nylon and shrugged off the harness. "Sorry it got messed up," he said.

I glanced at it. It wasn't so bad. "It's okay," I said. "You should see what Randy brings in. I think he tangles the lines on purpose."

Denny pulled at the lines and managed to untangle them. "You want to show me how to do this?" he asked. "Your dad said that everyone off student status should know how to do their own, and I only have one more jump, if I do okay."

"Going for number five today?"

"I wish, but I have to get back to town." He watched as I closed the pack of the rig I'd been working on. "So, okay if I give it a try?"

"You can help with the untangling as long as I'm the one who actually does the packing," I said. I pulled the slider out of the heap and started following one line after another, straightening each one out as I went.

Denny did the same, and as he ran his fingers up a line, his hand brushed mine. We both jumped, and Denny said, "Sorry" although he hadn't done anything to apologize for.

"It's okay," I said again, and then to cover up the awkwardness I said, "If you feel any roughness or see anything that looks like wear, let me know."

"Okay." He remained bent over the table, but I could see his ear, and it was pink.

When we had taken out all the tangles, I told Denny that I had to do the rest on my own, and then Noel came in and dumped three tandem rigs on the table. Being paid by the hour instead of by the rig wasn't cutting down on my workload any.

Denny said, "I'll let you get back to it. See you Saturday."

"Oh, you don't have to—" But he was gone.

It was almost two o'clock by the time I was able to stop for lunch, which was a leftover hot dog that I microwaved and wrapped in a piece of mushy white bread. I ate it standing up and then went back to the hangar.

Even when students came in jabbering and the Geezers told jokes, it seemed quiet without Denny. I listened to music, but my mind kept wandering. Denny wasn't as hot as Theo—he was shorter and much quieter, but he was definitely good-looking. He had such serious eyes, and the way his eyebrows arched over them . . . I turned up the volume on my iPod.

When we finally left for home, I reclined the passenger seat until I was almost lying down and said to my dad, "If I'm going to be on salary instead of piecework, I need to negotiate some breaks."

He glanced over at me and grinned. "Wiped out?"

"Um-hmm." I hoped he wouldn't ask me anything about the Travis incident. It was hard to lie to him, but if he figured out that I'd been the one driving, I'd be grounded forever.

"Staying home tonight, then?"

I nodded. It had been a long weekend—first, driving off the DZ without my dad knowing, then watching Travis nearly sizzle on the wires, and then Denny acting like touching me startled him. But I was so tired that instead of thinking, I fell asleep until we got home.

Julia came over and we watched some TV. She said Justin was being a jerk, so she was avoiding him.

"What did he do this time?" I asked, more because I had to than because I really was interested in the answer. In my opinion Justin was pretty much always a jerk, so when Julia got mad at him, I usually couldn't see what was so much worse than usual.

It turned out to be about canceling on her when something came up with his cousin. "He doesn't even *like* his cousin," Julia said.

"Maybe it was important to his parents," I said.

Julia shook her head and crunched a pretzel. "I think he just didn't feel like going out with me."

I didn't remind her that they spent most evenings and many days together and that *she* canceled on *him* all the time. Julia claimed to have abandonment issues because of the way her dad had left the family, and that when someone (especially Justin) did something that reminded her of that, it was hurtful. So all I said was, "Gives you and me some time together anyway, with Theo and Justin both deserting us."

"Would serve them right if we found someone else. Any hot prospects at the DZ?"

Even though I knew she was kidding, the question caught me off guard. After a pause I said, "No," but I knew my answer sounded fake.

Of course Julia caught it. She muted the TV and turned to me with a gleam in her dark eyes. "I don't believe you! Something's going on there. Spill!"

"What do you mean?" I asked. "Nothing's going on. I just—"

Julia wagged her finger at me. "Nuh-uh! You're turning red, and I can tell you're lying. What? Who? Is it Randy?"

I sighed, exasperated. Julia had been to the DZ a few times in the spring, and Randy had made a big play for her. She had said she wasn't interested, but afterward she asked about him a few times and said he was cute. "Of course it isn't Randy."

She pounced. "Aha! So there *is* someone! That photographer guy—Mad John?"

"Jack. Don't be crazy."

"The straight one of the twins?"

"No."

"A jump student?"

I didn't answer and she pounced again. "Ooh, Clancy, tell me!"

"There's nothing to tell." I sounded feeble, even to myself.

"Then why are you being so weird?"

I sighed. "I'm not being weird. I'm just tired. There's a new jump student named Denny and he's really nice, but that's all. I swear, Julia. I'm not interested in anyone but Theo. You know that."

"When the cat's away . . ." She raised her eyebrows at me meaningfully.

I couldn't help laughing at her; she looked like a little kid excited about a surprise.

"I swear, Jules, nothing has happened. No kiss, no flirting, no nothing. He's cute and all but he's just there to jump."

Julia looked skeptical, but the commercial ended and she unmuted the TV. I kept my phone on the coffee table but Theo didn't text.

I didn't hear from Theo again until Wednesday, and it was a phone call, not a text. He called while Julia was taking me home after we'd gone shopping. My dad had finally loosened up to the point where he'd let Julia drive me short distances during the day.

"Hey, Clance," Theo said. "I just wanted to hear your voice."

"Where are you?" I asked. "Theo," I mouthed at Julia.

"I have an afternoon off, so I'm in town doing laundry and catching up on things. My mom has emailed me every day, and she doesn't seem to get it that I can't read email at camp, so I just spent forever answering all her messages."

I let myself out of the car and waved good-bye to Julia, who said, "Say hi for me" and drove off.

I sat down on the porch steps. "Julia says hi."

"Say hi back."

"She left already."

Awkward silence.

"How's work?" Theo asked at the same moment that I said, "How's camp?" and again there was that silence.

Theo broke it with, "Really good." I waited for another long description of the rock climbing and the kids and the other counselors, but the silence stretched between us.

I finally said, "Julia's trying to quit her job already. Her mom's having a fit about it."

"Good old Jules." More silence.

"My dad put me on salary," I said. "He's paying me by the hour now, not by the rig."

"I know—you told me last time."

"Oh right."

Argh. Had we already run out of things to talk about? So I told him about Travis and his cross-country canopy ride even though Theo wasn't very interested in shoulda-died stories or student mishaps. "And Theo, guess what?"

"What?" He sounded distracted.

"My dad thinks that Den—that someone else drove and I just went along to navigate, but I was the one driving."

"Your dad let you drive off the DZ?"

Had he even been listening? "No, Theo," I said more sharply than I meant to. I softened my voice. "He thinks someone else was driving. He doesn't know it was me."

"Good thing it was a little country road on a weekend," he said.

Suddenly, I found it hard to breathe, like Theo and my dad were smothering me, and the images of the candlestick and the profiles flashed into my mind again. It seemed like it would be forever until I went away to college, to a place where no one would think I was either too ditzy to drive on a country road or too prudish to do anything even remotely edgy.

I stood up. "I've got to go. Thanks for calling."

"Miss me?"

"A ton." Suddenly, I meant it. We never had awkward silences when he was there in person, and he always paid attention to what I was saying. "When are you coming home?" I didn't care if I sounded needy.

"Not till the end of camp in August."

"You don't have any time between sessions or anything?"

"There's a break, but it's too short to drive all the way home and all the way back."

"I miss you." My voice caught.

"I know, sweetheart. I miss you too."

"I love you."

"Love you too. Bye."

I went into the house, where my dad was sitting at the sewing machine, finishing up the garish canopy he'd started the week before. "That might actually look okay, on second thought." I fingered the ripstop nylon. "I mean, it's not like canopies have to be subtle. And at least it'll be visible."

He grunted and finished a seam. "Done!" He stretched. "How's your classwork coming?"

"It's good. We're getting into the Renaissance." I found Renaissance art, with its emphasis on order and symmetry, much more satisfying than medieval art, where all sorts of odd things could pop up—three different parts of a saint's life all happening at the same time, perspective going off in wacky directions, strange critters poking their heads around columns in churches. Altogether too chaotic for me.

He glanced at the clock. "Yikes, look at the time. Can you put that stuff away?"

I gathered up the scraps of nylon, sorting out the pieces that were still large enough to use from the scraps to toss. "You going out?" I asked as he went into his room.

"Picking up some tools," he called back, "and then going to dinner at Elise's." He poked his head back through the door. "If you'll be okay on your own?"

"*Dad.* I've been old enough to legally babysit someone *else* for five years. Of *course* I'll be okay on my own."

The first time he had left me alone (which wasn't until I was almost fifteen), I'd noticed a lens poking out from the back of the bookcase. It was a nanny cam. I'd ripped it out of the wall and left it on the kitchen table where my dad would be sure to see it, along with a note saying that if he wanted me to run away, he should go ahead and install a new camera, because I refused to live with a father who spied on me. After he stopped freaking out about me running away, which I had to admit was just a threat, he used that line that all parents say: "It's not you I don't trust—it's other people."

"What other people?" I had said. "Julia's the only person who comes over, and we just watch TV and talk. If you don't trust Julia . . ." The nanny cam disappeared, and neither of us ever mentioned it again.

Now he asked, "Do you want to call Julia or someone to come over for dinner? I'll order you a pizza."

I shook my head. "I've got some things to do. You kids run along and have fun."

He grinned at me, and in a few minutes I heard the shower running. He'd call the landline on a flimsy pretext partway through his date, and I'd pretend not to know that he was checking up on me, but other than that I'd have some precious alone time.

After he left I tried to watch TV. I was too restless to concentrate on anything, so I turned it off after a few minutes and put on music way louder than my dad would have allowed. Something about that phone call with Theo had been . . . unsettling. I tried to tell myself it was just that I hadn't seen him in a long time, but it hadn't been that long.

On an impulse I sent Denny a text.

Me: How was the jump?

He answered almost immediately: Best yet. I did some 360s and didn't need any radio for the landing

Me: Did you stand it up?

Denny: Almost. Stumbled at the end

Me: Going again next weekend?

Denny: Bright and early Saturday morning!

Me: How are the monkeys?

Denny: Stinky. Obnoxious. Don't let anyone tell you monkeys are cute. They're mean. Class good?

Me: The usual

No response for a few minutes. Then he texted: What are you doing tonight?

Me: Not much. My dad went out

As I hit "send" it occurred to me that he might think saying I was alone was an invitation, so I hastily added, About to do some homework. Online test on Friday

Denny: How do they know you're not cheating?

Me: They don't. It's on the honor system. The tests don't count for anything. They're just practice so you know how you're doing

After a minute or so I read: You'll ace it. See you Saturday

Me: See you

How stupid was it that I got my feelings hurt that he didn't see my parentless state as an opportunity? *We're just DZ friends*, I told myself firmly. *Jump buddies*. I had never made a friend on the DZ that I also saw off-site, so this was nothing new. I told myself that I'd imagined the awkwardness when we touched accidentally. He hadn't been blushing—he was still on an adrenaline high from his jump, and that must have been why his ear was pink.

I scrubbed down the kitchen counters, which didn't need scrubbing, and organized the silverware drawer. Everything else was in perfect order, so I flopped down on the couch and tried to study.

Finally, I caved. I went into my room and sat down at my laptop. I had finally convinced my dad that Wi-Fi wasn't a luxury but a necessity, so I could have used it anywhere. But I needed the privacy of my room even though my dad wasn't home.

It had been a while—long enough that the link didn't autocomplete when I started typing it in the browser. While I hadn't been viewing the video, a few other people had. Not many, though. The numbers always spike after a skydiving accident, when people get ghoulish, but there hadn't been a fatality in the U.S. in ages. They always made the news. My dad said that if they reported on every jaywalker that was hit by a car, there wouldn't be anything but dead-jaywalker stories in the news, but let one jumper go in and it makes headlines.

The video started. I had seen it so many times that every little shake, every little pop in the low-quality audio was familiar. It was ominous too, like everything in the universe knew what was about to happen.

I paused the recording and slowly moved it forward, willing my mom to do something different. But what? She had cut away at exactly the wrong moment, but she had no way of knowing that it was going to *be* the wrong moment.

Jumpers try to avoid reserve rides, even though every instructor reminds students, "When in doubt, whip it out." It's not only the expense of paying a rigger to repack the reserve. Reserves open fast, and the hard opening can give you whiplash, but it's not the discomfort either. The main thing is that jumpers are superstitious. If you dump the reserve and it malfunctions too, you're sunk. Nowhere to go. Reserves just about never malfunction, and the odds against both the main and the reserve malfunctioning are astronomical, but still. . . .

So my mom had tried everything to clear the main. She did exactly what you're trained to do, exactly what I'd heard my dad and Leon and Noel and Randy and Louisa and Patsy tell their students: "If the pilot chute or the main canopy gets stuck, you have to break the burble." So she flipped over. It didn't work, so she flipped back to cut away, so the canopy would fly away cleanly. She had no way of knowing that the AAD would fire at precisely the wrong moment, making the two chutes—the main and the reserve—snag each other, and that neither one would open.

I watched to the end, seeing the pink canopy and the white one wrap around each other, making a big nasty barber pole that didn't slow my mom down enough to make a difference. Then, when Angie dropped the camera, the ground came up, up, up to the camera lens, and then— *whomp.* And the screen went black. *Was that the last thing my mom saw? The ground coming up, and then nothing? What did she think about in those last seconds? Did she think of me? Of my dad?*

After I went to sleep, I saw it over and over again, only sometimes she cut away sooner and sometimes she cut away later. But no matter what she did, it ended the same way, with the camera thumping on the ground and the sounds of screaming and crying.

I woke up when my dad got home, and I wanted to ask him to come sit by my bed until I fell asleep again. I wanted to tell him about how Theo was acting weird and how confused I was about Denny—about whether he was just a DZ friend or whether he was interested in me (and whether I was interested in him), and what I should do about it if he was. Or I was. I wanted to confess that I'd driven the car on Travis day and had done just fine.

I couldn't. He'd ground me forever. Anyway, he wasn't the sit-by-the-bed-until-you-fall-asleep kind of dad, and even if he were, once I got started, I'd tell him about watching the video. And seeing that we hadn't talked about my mom's death ever, not even once, I couldn't do that.

15

FACT: Freefall doesn't feel like falling to most sky-divers. Upon exiting the aircraft a skydiver travels forward at a high rate of speed, creating a sensation of solidity against the wind resistance, which the jumper also feels from below once she reaches terminal velocity (maximum speed downward). Sky-divers who jump from a fixed object (a cliff, bridge, etc.) or a hot-air balloon often experience initial disorientation due to the "softness" of the air.

—The Whuffo's Guide to Skydiving

"**A**re you saying you want to go to the DZ right after dinner?" My dad blinked at me over his newspaper as though the words I had spoken were incomprehensible. Which I guess they were, as this was the first time since I was twelve and had a crush on a jumper named Tad that I had wanted to leave for the DZ on a Friday. "Why?"

"There's nothing going on here tonight, and with Theo gone I don't have anything else to do. And this way I won't have to wake up at five a.m. I could roll out of bed, ready to pack, just as the first load is landing." I pushed the cereal around in my bowl, avoiding my dad's eyes. I wasn't really sure myself why I was eager to get there.

"You don't want to do something with Julia tonight?"

"I'm seeing her this afternoon, and then she and Justin are going out." Julia had forgiven Justin for whatever it was he had done and the two of them were spending every waking minute together (and some sleeping ones too, though my dad didn't need to know that), so as soon as he was off work, they'd be together. Most of my other friends were away for the summer or working. "So can we?"

He lowered his paper, looking uncomfortable. "Well, the fact is, I thought you'd be going out tonight, so I invited Elise over. She's going to teach me how to make lasagna. It would be rude for me to eat and run."

I was so startled that I couldn't think of what to say for a moment. "Oh, so you want me to clear out?"

"Well, that's not the way I'd put it. . . . "

"It's okay." I tried to hide my surprise. Dad taking cooking lessons. Dad wanting some time alone with a lady. Huh. "I'll see if Nicole or Cory or someone wants to go to a movie."

"You're sure? You could stay here and learn how to make lasagna too."

"Right, like that's what Elise is looking forward to—spending the evening with her date and his kid!" I laughed, and he smiled uncomfortably. "Fear not, revered sire. I'll get out of here. When's she coming?"

"She said six thirty, after work."

"Right. I'll be out by six."

"Be sure to tell me where you're going and who you're

going with. I'll call you after a while to make sure everything's okay." He went back to the newspaper, and then my phone pinged to tell me that Julia was outside.

As we walked to the park, where they had outdoor music on Friday afternoons in the summer, I told her about my dad and the cooking lesson. She glanced at me. "So are he and Elise serious?"

"I don't know. Is lasagna-making an accepted form of courtship?"

"Well, you know what goes with Italian food. Wine . . . candles . . . love songs playing in the background . . . " She let her voice trail off.

I tried again to imagine what it would be like if my dad got remarried, or even if he stayed with the same woman for more than a few months. It would be weird. But good weird or bad weird? He hadn't been serious about a woman since my mom died—at least as far as I knew, and given that we lived together in a tiny house, I'd probably know. I supposed I'd be glad if my dad was happy, and it would be nice to have his laser focus off me for a while, but it was still a strange thought.

"So what band is playing today?" I asked as we went through the park gate.

"Uh-uh. No changing the subject. Do you like her?"

I squirmed. "Yes. Sure. I guess so."

"Have you talked to your dad about her?"

"Not really." Unexpectedly, I felt a catch in my throat.

Julia patted my arm. "It's okay," she said softly. "But don't you think you should let him know how you feel?"

"We don't do that." Julia never got it. She and her mom and her sister, Celia, lived together in what my dad called the Estrogen Palace. They talked about their feelings a lot and sometimes got into fights that ended in tears and hugging. Julia didn't understand what it was like living with my dad, no matter how many times I told her that he might look tough but he got uncomfortable when I tried to talk about anything personal.

"Well, maybe you should." I followed her to the band shell, and we spent an hour on a blanket with lemonade and pretzels—our favorite snack since our first picnic together—listening to terrible music.

When Julia went to the Porta-John, I texted Nicole to see if she wanted to do something that night, but she was going dancing with friends. She invited me along, but I declined. I'd wind up getting no more than three hours' sleep, and I didn't want to be a zombie when I was packing the next day, even though I could probably do it in my sleep by now.

Just as I expected, everybody else was either out of town, unavailable, or doing something I would never be allowed to do. I was about to put my phone away when something occurred to me. Before I could lose my nerve, I texted Denny: What are you doing tonight?

Denny: Channel surfing. Chinese takeout. You?

Me: Want to try Mexican instead of Chinese?

A pause. Then: Sure. You mean that place you told me about?

Me: Manuelito's

If we took the time and effort to go out of town, Denny might think it was a date. Which it wasn't. Also, I figured if I took him to Manuelito's, no one who saw us would be suspicious, because if I was cheating, I wouldn't be so public about it. But if they happened to see me with Denny at some out-of-the-way place, they'd think I was hiding.

Clearly, I was overthinking the whole thing.

Denny: Sounds good. Meet there or should I pick you up?

Me: Better if you pick me up. I'm not home right now, but I'll be there by five

I would tell my dad this wasn't a date so he wouldn't think I was cheating on Theo. I'd remind him that Denny was new in town and I was just being friendly. I'd also tell him that Denny was eighteen, and he was in college, and that he and his father had rebuilt his car. That would be sure to impress my dad; he liked boys who did things like work on cars.

I finished texting Denny my address just as Julia came back. I hastily dropped my phone in my purse. I must have looked furtive, though, because once again, she pounced.

"How's Denny?" she asked.

"What makes you think I was texting Denny?"

My innocent act didn't work, and she teased me mercilessly all the way to the pool. We were spending the rest of the afternoon there to celebrate her last day of freedom. To my surprise and Julia's indignation, her mom had told her that far from being allowed to quit her part-time job at the miniature-golf place, Julie had to work full-time.

I thought her mom was probably sick of having her hanging around the Estrogen Palace all the time.

It was strange being at the pool without Theo. When he was lifeguarding I could feel his presence in the tall chair, even though he couldn't talk to me. After work he'd dive into the pool to cool off, and I loved watching him hoist his long, lean body out of the water, knowing that other girls were watching him and knowing that *I* was his girlfriend, not one of them.

Julia and I swam a few laps and then stayed in the shallow end, draped over floats. Since it was a weekday, there were mostly little kids and moms in the water, with lots of shrieking and calls of "Marco!" "Polo!" I left Julia with her float and swam more laps.

"I'm getting out," I told Julia when I passed her and went to stretch out on a chaise. She followed, toweling herself off. She wore a yellow bikini that fit her curves to perfection and showed off her brown skin, and the boys and few men there followed her with their eyes as she plopped herself down next to me.

"You're attracting attention," I told her as she lay back.

"Too bad Justin isn't here," she said. "A little jealousy is good for a guy."

"You think?" I always thought that making a guy jealous was childish, but what did I know? Whatever Julia and Justin were doing, it had worked for a long time. Theo and I had only been together for—I counted—almost five months. Maybe I could learn from her.

"Absolutely," she went on. "It might be really good for

your relationship with Theo if you dropped some hints about Denny."

"There's nothing to drop hints *about*."

She sighed theatrically. "I don't believe you, but even if you're telling the truth, there's no harm in making Theo think there *is* something going on."

"I don't see why, and besides, it's childish to play games."

"Oh, but playing games is fun! Why do you think they call it playing? Everyone does it anyway, and besides, it works. Men don't know what they've got until they think they're going to lose it."

I propped myself up on one elbow and looked at her. "And you like that? When they get territorial?"

She shaded her eyes with one hand and looked back at me. "You bet. Don't you?"

I lay back and considered this. "I guess I don't like to think of myself as territory to be defended."

"You know what I mean," she said. "It's nice to feel like you belong together and that he doesn't like the thought of you being interested in someone else. Don't you think?"

"Sure." I didn't feel like arguing. "I'm getting a snack. You want something?"

We had some chips and soda and went back in the water a few times, and then we walked back to my house and Julia drove home.

I couldn't wait to take off my clammy suit and get in the shower. But I had to wait, as it turned out. My dad was shaving in the bathroom, so I stripped off my suit in my room and put on my bathrobe. The smell of chlorine filled the tiny space. When we first moved to this house right before I started kindergarten, it had been plenty big, even with three of us. Now the two of us barely fit.

I checked texts and email. Denny said he'd see me soon.

I hoped he hadn't left yet. I went and pounded on the bathroom door. "Dad! I need to get ready to go out!"

"Hold your horses," he called through the door.

"If you don't hurry up, I'll still be here when you and Elise are cooking," I threatened.

"Heaven forbid," he said in mock terror, and in a minute he was out and I could finally wash off the pool water.

I was still drying my hair when the doorbell rang. I hadn't had a chance to tell my dad that Denny was picking me up, and it was strange that when I'd said I was going out, he hadn't asked me where I was going, who I was going with, and when I was going to be back. *He must really like Elise.*

I turned off the hair dryer and heard my dad's footsteps heading toward the door. I groaned. I hoped he wouldn't say anything stupid. It wasn't like Denny and I were going on a date. For all I knew, Denny had a girlfriend back home, or he was already seeing someone from his lab. We had never talked about that kind of thing.

I couldn't get from the bathroom to my room without being seen from the den, so I figured I might as well get my hair and makeup done before coming out. Denny had only seen me in DZ mode, and for once I wanted to look decent in front of him. "Be right out!" I called to my dad, to Denny, to both of them, I guessed, and hurried. I didn't want my dad to get chatty and say something about me being in high school, or even worse, about Denny driving to pick Travis up. Or worse still, about Theo. When I was done, I tightened the belt on my bathrobe and came out.

They were sitting in the den, talking. Denny glanced up at me, and he didn't have a terror-stricken look. My dad must not have been doing his usual interrogation about how long Denny had been driving or lecturing him about drinking and driving, and then giving Denny his cell number "in case of problems." And he wasn't glowering, so Denny must not have mentioned that I'd been the driver on Travis day. Phew.

"Sorry," I said. "My dad was hogging the bathroom." I made a face at my dad and he made one back. Phew again. He was in a good mood. "I'll just be another minute."

Denny stood up when I came back. "Ready?"

I flashed him a smile. "Finally, right? Sorry," I said again. "Bye, Dad. Have fun!"

Denny reached the door first and held it for me, and I ran down the steps before my dad could call me back on some pretext and either grill me about Denny or lecture me about being careful.

As I settled into the passenger seat, I realized that I should have noticed before that this car wasn't some rich kid's graduation present. There was no new-car smell and the upholstery was worn. "What were you and my dad talking about?" I asked.

"Mostly about the lab. He was interested in what I did there and what I was going to study."

"Did you tell him psych?"

"I said pre-med. It's close enough and parents always like it."

"Turn right," I directed, and for the rest of the drive I showed him my personal landmarks. We passed the church where my Girl Scout troop used to meet. I told him that Angie had told my dad I needed female role models who didn't jump out of airplanes, so he put me in Brownies the next day. Then came the house where my first best friend, Alex, had lived until she moved to Michigan right before I met Julia; next was my old elementary school, where some boys were shooting hoops next to the swing set that Theo and I had played on right before he left for Idaho. I felt myself flush when I glimpsed the path leading to the passion pit and wished I had left the playground out of the tour. I kept my face turned away from it and pointed out a supposedly haunted house.

We passed the big brick high school. Denny said it looked like something out of an old TV show. In another minute we reached town, if you could call it that. "You can park anywhere," I told him.

Inside Manuelito's I looked around for a table. No luck. In fact, there was a line inside the door. I groaned and turned to Denny. "Want to try someplace else?"

"I was all set for Mexican." He surveyed the crowd. "Is there another Mexican place in town?"

"Nope. Not unless you count drive-throughs."

"How about this—let's get something to go, and we'll have a picnic?"

"Good idea. I recommend the flautas." I pulled a menu out of its holder at the hostess station.

We ordered, and then I wasn't surprised when Julia's familiar voice called my name. She and Justin were sitting in the back. I waved, but I knew she wouldn't let me get away with that, and sure enough she gestured at me to come over.

"I need to go say hi to my friends," I said, but instead of waiting for me, Denny came along.

"Denny, these are Julia and Justin." Julia's eyes sprung wide at the name, and she looked meaningfully from me to him and back to me again. I ignored her, though my face turned hot. "Denny's doing an AFF course at my dad's drop zone."

"What's AFF?" Justin asked, and while Denny was explaining, Julia beckoned me to lean over.

"Cuuuute," she said under cover of the conversations and music.

"Jules, *please* don't say anything about Theo, and don't let Justin either. Denny doesn't—"

"Do you think I'm stupid? Of course I won't."

"And don't say anything to Theo either. Denny's just a friend."

"Mm-hmm."

"And Julia . . . " I leaned in closer. "He thinks I'm in college, so don't say anything about school, okay?"

"But he's just a friend, hmm?" She cocked her head and grinned.

"Seriously, Julia—"

"Clancy, they're calling our order." Denny was a lot closer

than I had thought, and I fervently hoped he hadn't over-heard us.

"We've got to go." I forced a smile at Julia and Justin. "See you."

"Get it while it's hot!" Julia said, and Justin winked at me. I wished the two of them would cut it out. I waved and followed Denny back to the takeout counter. He was taking his wallet out.

"Hey, *I* invited *you*," I protested. "I'm paying. Anyway, you paid for lunch last weekend. And you had to drive all the way here."

"No way," Denny said. "You rescued me from ramen noodles for dinner."

"I thought you said Chinese takeout."

"I was trying to impress you. I thought takeout didn't sound as pathetic as ramen."

"Let's at least split it." We paid, and I felt Julia's eyes on me as we left, but I didn't turn around.

I must have exhaled louder than I meant to when we got outside, because Denny looked at me curiously. "Problem?"

"I don't care if she's my best friend," I said. "Sometimes I could *kill* her."

He unlocked the driver's side door. "Best friends do that to you. Sometimes I could kill Frederick too." He pulled up the lock on the passenger door. After I sat down, he handed me the food bags. They were so hot I had to hold them off my lap as I directed him to a picnic area in the park next to the playground, the one farthest away from the passion pit.

"How's Frederick doing, anyway?" I asked.

"Not so good. They've pumped him full of steroids because of the graft-versus-host thing and it makes him jumpy. Plus, he's covered in hives and they're really itchy. His mom couldn't even talk to me about it, she was so upset. His brother texted me."

I didn't know what to say. On an impulse I reached over and put my hand on top of his, where it rested on his thigh. His leg twitched a little, and then he turned his hand palm up and held mine until he had to shift gears.

I chose a spot that was in the open so that Denny wouldn't think I was taking him to a private area on purpose. We sat down on a bench near the pond, but as soon as the ducks saw us, they bustled out of the water and ran at us, their tails waggling and their beaks open. They made an awful noise, and I knew they wouldn't let us eat in peace. We grabbed our paper bags and ran back to the car just ahead of them. "So where to now?" Denny asked as the disappointed ducks waddled back down to the water, complaining loudly.

"There are more tables around that way." He drove where I pointed. A family was at the next picnic area, grilling something while three kids ran around playing, so we kept going until we finally found a vacant one tucked under a big tree. It was more secluded than I'd been aiming for, but it would have to do.

One of the Manuelito's bags had gotten wet and was starting to split, so we unloaded it carefully. Denny had flautas and a taco, and I had flautas and chile relleno. There were chips and salsa, a lot of napkins, and two Cokes. Mine was marked for no ice, which was convenient because the ice in Denny's had long since melted. "See?" I said. "Another advantage of Coke *sans* ice. They're both lukewarm now, but yours is lukewarm *and* watered down."

"I bow to your superior Coke knowledge. From now on, no ice for me either." He held up his cup, and I touched mine to it.

We didn't talk a lot while we ate. "Like it?" I wiped my mouth.

"Umph. *Tons* better than ramen. You were right about the flautas. But there was too much." He untangled his legs from the picnic-table bench and started to sit on the grass.

"Don't!" I warned him. "Chiggers!"

He paused. "What's that?"

"You don't have them in Colorado?"

"Never heard of them. What are they?"

"Microscopic little bugs that itch worse than a mosquito bite. And they always seem to bite you in places you can't scratch in public."

He looked around. "But if I don't lie down, I'll burst!"

I patted the picnic table. "They can't jump." He looked dubious, like he thought I was kidding about the chiggers, but he lay down on his back on the table. I joined him, keeping a careful distance between us. We lay in silence for a few minutes.

"So why skydiving?" I asked him.

"What do you mean?"

"Why didn't you and Frederick plan to go bungee

jumping or hang gliding or scuba diving or something? I mean, there are lots of ways to get a thrill."

"I guess we figured bungee jumping was something you did once just to say you did it. Every bungee jump you do after that would be the same as the first one. And scuba diving—you can kind of ease into it by snorkeling or something, you know? But from your very first jump, skydiving is all or nothing. You can keep doing it, and then when you're good, it becomes like a sport."

"Not *like* a sport," I corrected him. "It is a sport. It takes lots of skill."

"Oh, you don't have to convince *me* of that! I can't believe how much Louisa and Randy can do in freefall. I'd like to be able to do even half of that someday."

"So you'll keep coming to Knoxton?"

"At least this summer," he said. "I don't know how much time I'll have once school starts."

"Oh, come on," I said. "I need you out there to keep me from going crazy."

"Packing rigs all summer isn't your idea of fun?"

"It's not bad," I said. "There are worse jobs, even if they don't involve monkey poop."

He groaned. "Don't remind me! But at least there are interesting people at the DZ. Cynthia's cool, and I like Louisa. And I can tell how much you like Randy."

"Oh yes," I said. "I *love* Randy. I just wish I loved him half as much as he loves himself. But it gets old spending all summer with my dad."

He turned to face me and propped himself up on one

elbow. "You could make a jump to pass the time, you know."

That was so unexpected that I didn't know what to say. Denny waited, but when I didn't answer, he said, "Is it really your dad, or do you not want to?"

"I don't know if I want to. I've always felt like it was something that wasn't open to me, you know? So I haven't even thought about it. It's like . . ." I tried to think of something to compare it to. "It's like if you had, I don't know, diabetes and you didn't know whether you didn't want ice cream because you knew you couldn't, or because you really didn't want it. I'm sorry, that makes no sense. But it's kind of like I have no-jump syndrome, and I can't tell if—"

"Because if it's only because of your dad," Denny said, "why don't you make a jump someplace else?"

16

Kiss pass: A kiss exchanged between two jumpers in freefall. A kiss pass does not necessarily imply romantic involvement.

—*The Whuffo's Guide to Skydiving*

"**M**ake a jump someplace else?" I sat up.

"Why not?" Denny stared up at the sky, his arms behind his head. "That other place, the Jump Ranch . . . it isn't too far away, right? And you already know all about jumping and the safety procedures, right? From watching all those classes? It's like you already took the class a hundred times. So if the planes are okay, like you said they were, it should be just as safe as Knoxton."

It was very simple why I couldn't make a jump someplace else. I'd have to prove I was eighteen, even at the loosey-goosey Jump Ranch, and when I couldn't, they wouldn't let me make a jump, not even a tandem. *Maybe I should tell Denny how old I really am,* I thought. It was bound to come out sometime, like if someone at the DZ said something to me about going back to Hawkins High or asked if I was thinking about where I was going to apply to college.

"I'm not . . ." But I stopped. The problem was that I liked Denny thinking I was older than I was. I liked the way he treated me, as though I could take care of myself without a big strong man to protect me.

"You're not what?"

"I'm not sure I want to."

He propped himself up on his elbows. "Really?"

I thought about my observer ride with Norton, and how much fun it had been to play in the clouds. I thought of the whoops and hollers of students as they landed, how their faces were shiny, how they felt triumphant, even though with a tandem jump they hadn't really done anything.

"If you decide you want to," Denny said, "just let me know. I'll drive you out there."

"Ha! If only my dad could hear you. He talks about the Jump Ranch like it was some . . . I don't know, den of iniquity or something. I always picture it like a place in one of those old movies where you have to do a special knock and say a password before they'll let you in, and it's all smoky and murky."

"And the planes are held together with duct tape, and the boss smokes a big cigar."

"And here you are, offering to take me to that evil place! You must be evil too."

He grinned up at me, and before I knew I was going to do it, I leaned forward and kissed him, just a quick brush on the lips. I started to pull back, embarrassed, but his hand was on the back of my head, twining in my hair, and he gently pulled my face down and kissed me back. The tip of his tongue flicked my lips, and I parted them and leaned into him. His arms went around me, and then I was lying next to him, and he was kissing me on the chin, the neck, behind my ear.

I had never really kissed anyone except Theo, not counting Cory in sixth grade and kissing games at parties, and this was different. I opened my eyes. Denny was looking at me. He pulled back a little and smiled.

"What?" I asked.

He drew me close and whispered in my ear, "Do you know how long I've wanted to do that?"

"No. How long?"

He looked up and squinted, and his lips moved like he was pretending to count. "Since I first saw you in the hangar after my tandem jump."

"Oh, and from the way you talked that day, I thought you were disappointed that I wasn't a guy!"

"Not disappointed." His hand circled my waist. "No, that's not the word I'd use. Especially the way your shirt, um, hung open when you leaned over."

I was glad it was dark and he couldn't see my face.

"I was intimidated, though," Denny said.

"Intimidated? By me?"

"You were so sure of yourself, so confident. You packed

rigs as easily as someone else folds a T-shirt, and they were all perfect. You seemed to know exactly what you want to do with your life—"

"Oh right, and you tried to shoot down my archaeology plans!" I laughed, and he laughed a little too.

"I wasn't shooting them down," he protested. "I wanted to know why you were interested in it. And there I was, all dorky and excited from jumping out of a plane tied up to someone like a . . . like a turkey, acting like I was the one who had done something. But there you were—"

"All sweaty and dusty—"

He laughed. "If you had any idea how beautiful you look all sweaty and dusty!" And he kissed me again.

After a while my phone pinged. "Oh crud." I started to push myself up to sitting.

"Just leave it." He kissed me again and for a moment I was tempted.

"I can't." I wriggled out of his arms and sat up. I swiped my hair back off my face. "It might be my dad. If I don't answer, he'll send out a search party."

My heart thudded when I saw it was Theo. He texted that he'd gotten the evening off and was with some other counselors in town, and could I call him? Hoping Denny couldn't see my face, which I knew had to be beet red, I typed quickly and then said, "I've got to go."

"Was that your dad?"

I hesitated. Then, "No. But he'll be wondering where I am. I just told him dinner." I stood up. He didn't. "Denny, I really have to get back."

"Was it your boyfriend?"

I stared at him. When I tried to speak, he said, "It's okay. I should have asked before I kissed you."

"For the record," I said, "you didn't kiss me. I kissed you."

"I kissed you back. And I want to kiss you again. But if you have a boyfriend . . ." I didn't answer. "Do you?"

I nodded.

"High-school sweetheart?"

I nodded again. "But he's away for the summer. And we've been . . ." I hesitated, and then finished, "We've been kind of growing apart lately."

Denny stood. His hair was mussed. "Come on. I'll take you home." He didn't sound angry, and he held out a hand to help me up. I took it but let go as soon as I was standing.

We rode in silence. As he pulled up to the curb in front of my house, I said, "I'm sorry."

"Sorry for what?"

"That I didn't tell you about—Theo." I had to force the name out. "About my boyfriend."

"It's okay, Clancy." For the first time I heard something in his voice, hurt or irritation or impatience. "When the cat's away, right?"

"It's not like that! I didn't tell you because I didn't think it mattered. I thought we were friends, hanging out together. It's not like I planned to kiss you. It just happened, that's all. And then you kissed me back and I—"

"If I'd known about the boyfriend, I wouldn't have."

"Are you sorry you did?" I didn't mean to sound accusatory, but that's how it came out.

"I should probably say yes. But I'm not. And I should probably say I'm not coming out to the DZ again. I know Frederick's parents would understand if I stopped. Frederick would too, but I'll be there tomorrow. I'll try to stay out of your way."

"Okay," I whispered. I started to get out.

"Just one thing," he said. "I don't want to break you and your boyfriend up. But be more honest with him than you were with me, okay?"

"Okay," I said again. This time I didn't manage to hold back the tears, and I ran into the house.

My dad and Elise were still at the table, and the house smelled of garlic and tomatoes and cheese. I called, "Hi!" and waved as I headed to my room. I hoped they wouldn't stop me and make me talk. I closed my door and called Theo.

I got his voice mail. I guessed he had gone out of cell range again. "Damn it!" I had to stop myself from throwing the phone against the wall. I suddenly, desperately needed to hear Theo's voice. I wanted to hear him say he loved me and missed me, and that the rock-climbing girl wasn't important. I told myself that was all I needed, that I had kissed Denny only because I was lonely and insecure, and that if Theo hadn't been so hard to reach, I would never have done it.

But I couldn't explain away the flip of my stomach when I remembered kissing Denny.

A knock came at the door. "You want some dessert?"

It was Elise. I wanted to ignore her but couldn't bring myself to be that rude, so I said, "You can come in."

Elise opened the door and poked her head in. She held out a plate with something white and brown on it. "Tiramisù. From the Italian bakery in my neighborhood."

I stood up and took it from her. "Thanks." She still stood there. "Want to come in?"

"If you're sure I'm not intruding." She barely stepped inside the door, and her eyes swept the room. "I must say, if I had kept my things half this neat when I was your age, my mother would have been one happy woman."

"I like everything to be in order." I tried not to sound stiff.

"I can tell." She hesitated. "You okay?"

"I'm fine. Why?"

She motioned at the mirror. I looked into it and groaned. "Terrific." My eyes were red. Also, my makeup was smeared, and the beginnings of a hickey showed on my neck.

"Your dad didn't notice," she assured me. "The dessert was an excuse to let you know so you could, um, take care of things before you come out again."

"Thanks," I said. "I really appreciate it."

She put her hand on the doorknob and paused. "You might want to brush your hair while you're at it." I put my hand on the back of my head and found that it was all mussed from the picnic table.

"Thanks," I said again.

Her hand still rested on the doorknob, but she didn't leave. "You okay?" she repeated.

I forced a smile and said as dismissively as I could manage, "Oh, just a little guy trouble," but my voice trembled.

Elise crossed the room and was holding me almost before I knew it. She gave me a good firm hug, rubbing my back. I found myself hugging her too, and a little of the tension I'd been holding melted as I relaxed into her.

After a minute she loosened her grasp and stepped back. "Your dad told me about your boyfriend getting that job out of the blue," she said. "Is that the problem?"

"Part of it," I said, and I don't know whether I was relieved or disappointed that she didn't press me for details.

"It's tough," she said. "I know how hard it can be."

"Elise?" my dad called from the den.

"Be right there," she called back.

"Don't say anything to him," I begged her.

"I wouldn't," she assured me. "Just don't get too bent out of shape about it, okay? And let me know if you want to talk sometime." She scribbled on the notepad on my desk. "My phone number. Whenever." This time she did leave, closing the door behind her.

I tried to tell myself that it wasn't a big deal, that people hugged each other all the time, but I knew this actually was kind of a big deal. I had never hugged any of Dad's girlfriends before.

I heard my dad say something to her—I couldn't make out the words—and she laughed. Then dishes clattered in the kitchen. For a moment I thought of going out there and joining them, and maybe trying to get Elise alone so I could tell her what had happened. I even got up and headed to my bedroom door, but I chickened out and turned back.

So I set the plate on my bedside table and went into

the bathroom while they were still doing the dishes. It was early, but after I got cleaned up, I crawled into bed with my laptop and watched old sitcoms until I heard Elise leave. I fell asleep but kept waking up.

The next morning, it was still dark when I heard my dad moving around in the kitchen.

The day started out foggy again, but something about the light coming through the mist told me that it would clear soon. We were almost at Knoxton when my dad broke the silence. "Denny jumping today?"

I was slumped in the passenger seat, watching the air brighten as the sun did its work and lifted the fog. "He said he was."

"Nice guy."

I grunted.

"Not as nice as Theo," my dad said.

I refused to let him draw me into a discussion about the relative merits of my boyfriend and my—what? Was Denny my friend, or had I ruined that the night before? So I changed the subject. "How was your date?"

"Good. Now I can make two different dinners. Beef Stroganoff and lasagna." Even though I was still looking out the window, I could feel him glance at me. "Elise wants to sign us up—her and me—for cooking classes."

"Really?" *My dad in cooking classes?*

We pulled into the lot. Denny's red sports car wasn't there. Not knowing—once again—whether I felt relieved or disappointed, I went into the hangar. Pretty soon jumpers were showing up, and I got busy. I packed all day and didn't take a lunch break, even though my dad remembered our talk about having regular breaks and told me to stop for a while. I said I would, but I didn't. We had reheated lasagna for dinner, and then someone made s'mores. I forced one down and listened to the jumpers analyze what they'd done that day. As soon as I could, I told my dad I had a headache and fell asleep in my clothes in the trailer. I didn't wake until dawn on Sunday.

Cynthia seemed to know something was up. "You okay, sweetie?" she asked when I went into the office to make coffee.

I nodded and watched the coffeepot fill up. Behind me Cynthia said, "Dang it!"

"What?" I didn't really care; I just wanted her not to ask me what the matter was.

"We're almost out of that heavy paper for printing first-jump certificates on, and we have a lot of students scheduled today. I don't have time to get it. Can you see if your dad will let you go to town when the Mart opens?"

"You bet."

I carried my coffee into the hangar and texted Angie: You busy? Can I call?

There was nothing for me to pack yet. While I waited for Angie to answer, I poked around restlessly and paged through the *National Geographic* magazine I'd left on my shelf. I couldn't concentrate on it.

My phone dinged. Angie: Not a good time. Both kids have strep. Just shoot me. I'll call when I can. I tossed my phone on the shelf, biting my lip in frustration. *Elise?* But I hadn't added her to my contacts, and the paper with her number written on it was still on my desk at home.

Margaret Finnegan's logbook caught my eye, and I remembered that I had meant to take it to Cynthia. I stuck it in my bag along with my phone so I wouldn't forget again. I flipped through "The Whuffo's Guide to Skydiving," which started with entries written in my careful little-girl handwriting.

"Hey." It was Denny. I looked up from my notebook. He was standing in the doorway, a rig dangling from his hand.

"Hey," I said back. It was the best I could do. I couldn't see his face clearly, with the light behind him. I didn't ask him where he'd been the day before. I didn't want to hear the answer.

"I'm going up on the first load." So he didn't want to talk about Friday night, or maybe he was waiting for me to bring it up. Which I didn't know how to do.

"Have fun." My voice was husky, and I cleared my throat. I turned my back to the door and pretended to be fascinated by my "Whuffo's Guide." When I figured he had left, I exhaled. Then I felt a touch on my shoulder, and I turned around. He was right there, his serious golden eyes fixed on me.

"I couldn't sleep Friday night," he said.

"Me either. Oh, Denny, I'm so sorry. I really messed up."

Then his arms were around me and he was kissing me—sweet, gentle kisses, not like before. Tears spilled out of my eyes and he kissed them off my cheeks. I pulled away and ripped a paper towel off the holder and blew my nose.

"Did you talk to him?" he asked.

"Theo? No, he can't use his cell. He's out in the wilderness."

"What are you going to tell him?"

"I don't know." I felt tears threatening again. "I don't know how I feel. I need to see him to figure it out."

"When will that happen?"

A deep voice came from behind Denny. "How about right now?"

I jumped away from Denny, who spun around. There in the doorway stood a tall, familiar figure.

Theo.

17

Hypoxia: The state of being deprived of oxygen. Sufferers show agitation, confusion, and shortness of breath.

—The Whuffo's Guide to Skydiving

All I could do was blink. My first impulse was to run out of the hangar, but I forced myself to stay. "What—what are you doing here?" I stammered. "How did you get here?"

"I drove," Theo said grimly. "I have a long weekend off between sessions. I left yesterday and came straight here."

"Why didn't you tell me you were coming?"

"Good thing I didn't." He glared at Denny and then back at me. "I wanted to surprise you. Don't you know what today is?"

I stared at him, confused. It wasn't my birthday and it wasn't his birthday. "What?"

"Our five-month anniversary."

"It is?" I counted in my head. "Oh shit. It is."

"Not the reaction I was hoping for."

"I think I'd better leave you two alone." Denny edged toward the door.

"Maybe you should," I said, but Theo blocked his path.

"Not so fast. Who are you?"

"Theo—" I started.

"Be quiet, Clancy," he snapped. Always the gentleman. Anyone else would have said "Shut up."

"Dennis Rider," Denny said. "I'm a jump student. And you're the boyfriend, I take it."

"That's right. So if you're jumping, you're at least eighteen, am I right?" He didn't wait for an answer. "Don't you have anything better to do than pick up high-school girls?"

I looked from tall, glowering Theo to short, bewildered Denny. "You're in high school?" Denny asked me. "I thought you were in college!"

I shook my head.

"But you told me—"

"I didn't tell you I was in college. You assumed it, and I let you go on believing it." I knew this was feeble, and from the look on Denny's face he knew it too. I wished so hard that I had been truthful from the beginning.

"She's sixteen," Theo snapped.

Denny said slowly, "So the article about your mom . . . where it said she had a six-year-old daughter, they got that right? I thought the reporter . . ."

"A sixteen-year-old is jailbait," Theo told him. "The age of consent in Missouri is seventeen."

"The age of—" I felt my mouth hanging open and shut it. "Theo, did you think—" I choked, and couldn't finish.

Denny was the reddest I'd ever seen him. "You've got it all wrong," he said, "but I don't need to justify myself to you." He headed for the hangar door again, but Theo blocked him and shoved him in the chest.

"You think because you're a rich kid you get to steal people's girlfriends, do anything you want?" Theo demanded.

Denny looked at me. "Do you feel stolen?"

"Leave her out of this," Theo snarled. "This is between you and me."

"Clancy too, I think," Denny said mildly. "And not that it matters, but I'm not a rich kid."

"Clancy's a lady." Theo was still glaring at him. "She doesn't get involved in this, do you hear me? We can settle it between us."

The way Theo was acting made any feeling of guilt about kissing Denny shrivel up and die. I finally found my voice. "There's nothing to settle. You're acting like an idiot, Theo."

"*I'm* acting like an idiot? I drive all the way home to surprise you, and I find you with this guy that you didn't even know a few weeks ago, and you tell me there's nothing going on and expect me to believe it?"

"I think you drove back here because Justin told you I was at Manuelito's with Denny. That's why you texted me and wanted to talk, isn't it? Anyway, you know I hate surprises; I've told you that a hundred times."

He rolled his eyes. "Not this again."

Suddenly I had to get out of there. "You know what? I'll just go now. I don't want to be in the same place as you—I don't even want to breathe the same air as you." I was getting woozy from hyperventilating. "Denny, I'm really sorry this happened. It's not your fault. It's mine."

"Where are you going?" Theo asked.

"Cynthia needs something in town," I snapped. I started to leave, when something struck me. I turned back. "You drove all night to come here and surprise me?"

Theo nodded.

"You didn't stop at home to change or take a nap or anything? You were so eager to see me that you came straight here?"

He nodded again, but I recognized a guilty look on his face. Something was fishy. Theo hated the DZ, and he never came out here. Besides, neither one of us had even noticed when our four-month anniversary came and went—would he really drive all the way here for our fifth? Our sixth, maybe, but not fifth. Plus, he knew I'd be working and that even if my dad wanted to let me take time off, he couldn't, not on a day like this, when students were bound to be lining up.

"I'll just leave you two alone," Denny said again. This time Theo moved aside and let him go.

"Do you have something to tell me?" I asked when we were alone. Theo avoided my gaze. "Something about a girl? Another girl?" At each question he flinched, but I felt no mercy. "The rock-climbing girl—the one in the picture?"

At last he looked at me, and his dark eyes were misty with tears. "I'm sorry. I didn't mean to hurt you."

"You haven't hurt me yet," I said, although I knew he was about to.

He took a deep breath. "Ali—the rock-climbing girl—she's . . . I'm . . . we've been seeing each other."

"You mean sleeping together." *Please deny it*, I begged silently.

But he didn't. Instead, he said, "She's . . . different from you." I waited. "She's brave, she takes risks. She doesn't need someone to protect her."

"Sh-she d-doesn't need—" I sputtered. I made myself breathe. "*She* doesn't need someone to protect her? Neither do I! I keep telling you and my dad to back off, that I can take care of myself, and you both ignore me! And now you're *punishing* me for it? For your own fantasy that I need you?" My voice had risen, and I clamped a hand over my mouth to hold in a sob. The last thing I wanted was for my dad to hear me and come in.

I spoke through my trembling fingers. "And you come back here and accuse me of . . . and all the while, *you're* the one . . . with that rock-climbing girl . . . " Everything I felt—rage, hurt, the last shred of guilt—threatened to choke me, and I couldn't speak. Half-blinded by tears, I stumbled out of the hangar and into the office. Cynthia, blessedly, was on the phone and didn't look up as I grabbed my dad's keys off the hook.

Out in the parking lot, I heard someone running behind me. I turned, ready to tell Theo to back off. But it was

Denny. "Clancy, wait! You shouldn't drive when you're mad. Can't you wait till you've cooled down? I'd take you myself wherever it is you're going, but I don't want him to think I'm running away from him."

"I'm okay, Denny," I managed to say. "I'll be careful, I promise. Cynthia wanted me to get something at the Mart, and I need to get out of here for a while. There's nothing to crash into between here and Knoxton." I glanced back at the hangar and saw Theo heading toward the Porta-Johns. He hadn't even stopped to pee? He'd been in that much of a hurry to confront me? And then when he heard me talking to Denny he turned all his guilt about Ali into anger at me.

"Sure?" Denny asked uncertainly. I nodded. "Okay, then. I'll go back and try to convince him that nothing happened between us."

"Don't bother," I said. "I don't care what he thinks happened. I never want to see him again." I really didn't. The way he had cheated and lied—it was infuriating and humiliating.

Cynthia's voice boomed out of the PA system, calling the next load, which Denny was on. "You have to go too," I said.

"Okay." He sounded unconvinced, and he glanced back at me as he walked across the landing area toward the plane.

Then I remembered my driver's license. I wasn't likely to be pulled over on the Knoxton road on a Sunday morning, but the last thing I needed today was a ticket. I went back into the hangar, hoping that Theo would still be in the Porta-John. He wasn't anywhere to be seen, so I retrieved my purse.

It was heavier than usual with Margaret Finnegan's logbook inside it.

I froze in place. I'd had a thought, a crazy thought that swirled up out of the ache in my chest and the turmoil in my mind. It was just a tiny idea, and I didn't know exactly how I was going to do it, but I knew I'd figure it out.

The Geezers were the only jumpers in the hangar, and they were still being discreet and ignoring me. I took a breath and quietly opened my cashbox. I took out a handful of folded bills and slid them into my pocket.

I got into the car and sat folded over for a moment with my eyes closed, my forehead against the steering wheel. My dad would be disappointed in me; he'd say I should have broken up with Theo before getting involved with Denny. He would be right, but it's not like I'd planned any of that. And he'd be sure to find out about me driving to Knoxton today without checking with him. He'd clamp down, and I'd be so stifled I'd explode.

I had to get out of there, off the DZ, and go—where? Angie was hundreds of miles away. My dad's parents were dead. I hardly knew my mom's parents, and they lived in California anyway. My dad would have the National Guard out looking for me before I'd gone fifty miles.

I started the car and backed out slowly. There was nothing I could do, nowhere I could go. That little idea I'd had back in the hangar was nuts. I'd buy Cynthia's paper at the Mart, and when I came back Theo would be gone, and Denny would be making a jump or driving back to his monkeys.

Only that's not what I did.

I drove through town without stopping at the Knoxton Mart and kept going until I pulled into the parking lot of the Jump Ranch.

\\\\\\\\\\\

After what my dad had said about the rival DZ, I'd expected derelict old aircraft and tumbledown buildings. Instead, it looked okay. Small, and maybe not as well kept as Skydive Knoxton, with weeds growing out of cracks in the runway and some rust spots on the hangar's metal roof, but the aircraft—two Cessna 182s—looked fine from what I could see, and Norton had said they were well maintained. Four jumpers were dirt diving with all the seriousness and precision of anyone at Knoxton. With a lot more seriousness and precision than some of the Knoxton jumpers actually, the Geezers in particular.

I watched the jumpers through my windshield. I didn't know any of them. I took a deep breath and stepped out. I hadn't seen Raymond, who owned the DZ, for a few years, and I didn't think he'd recognize me.

They didn't have a for-real office, just a chair in the doorway of the hangar in front of a card table with a metal cashbox and a legal pad on it, and a guy with a gray beard sitting there. "Morning," he said as I approached.

"Hey." My palms were sweaty. "I, um, I did an AFF class at Knoxton and got cleared for my solo. I was wondering if I could do it here." I laid Margaret Finnegan's logbook down on the table. Surely, this guy would figure that someone at Skydive Knoxton had verified my age, and he wouldn't bother doing it again; my dad was famous for being strict about things like that.

The guy flipped through the logbook. "It's been a while since your last AFF. Let me run this by the boss. He might want you to do a refresher before he lets you solo."

I bit back a protest. *Play it cool*, I told myself. I stretched my lips back in what I hoped was a smile and nodded. Carrying the logbook, the guy disappeared into the hangar. I strained unsuccessfully to hear what they were saying, and then the bearded guy came back out with a heavy man, shorter than my father, with a receding hairline. I recognized him from the DC-3 days.

"Margaret?"

I nodded.

He stuck out his hand. "Raymond Purvis. So you want to solo?"

"Yes, sir." I shook his hand, hoping he would put my sweaty palms down to the normal nerves of a jump student.

"Why not at Knoxton? That's where you did your AFF course, right?"

"It's too expensive there. My boyfriend paid for the classes, but then we broke up before I soloed, so . . . " I let my voice trail off.

"So you want to prove that you weren't just doing it for the boyfriend."

It wasn't really a question but I answered it. "Right." It was kind of true anyway.

"Good for you."

He was a nice man. This was something I hadn't figured into what little plan I'd made—that I'd be lying to a nice man. But I'd just make this one jump and leave, and he'd never find out that I had lied to him, that I wasn't Margaret Finnegan.

He glanced at the entries in Margaret's logbook. I'd already read them. She had done okay—a little hesitation on her first pull, but that was normal. She hadn't recorded her solo, where she had broken her ankle. "I don't know. I think I should have one of my instructors go out with you once, and then you can solo after that."

That was not in the plan either. If I was going to do this, I was going to do it right, meaning that nobody would be there to help me, not even an AFF instructor. I had to do it all by myself.

"I really can do it." I knew how feeble that sounded. "And I didn't bring enough money for an instructor."

"Tell you what. I'll take you out myself and give you a break on the price. You don't have your own rig, do you?"

I shook my head. Damn. I wished I'd thought to bring one; now I'd have to pay for a rental too.

He looked up and squinted while he mentally calculated the price of the jump, a discounted instructor fee, and a rig rental, and named a figure. "Can you handle that?"

I pulled the wad of bills out of my pocket and riffled through them. I nodded. "Just." An AFF with an instructor wasn't what I wanted, but at least I'd be doing everything on my own, even if Raymond was in the air with me.

While we'd been talking, two loads had gone up. Soon my dad would start wondering where I was. Cynthia would have told him about the paper, but going to the Mart wouldn't take more than an hour, and I'd already been gone almost that long.

"Can we go up soon?" I asked.

"I like that kind of enthusiasm!" he said. "Sure. Give Frank your money. He's about to go on break, so I'll get you a rig. Frank, this young lady and I will be going up on load three. Tell Hal to wait for us."

Now that I was about to go, I started to freak out that I'd have to jump a rig that someone else had packed. I paid the gray-bearded man and ran after Raymond. When I caught up to him, I asked, "Can I repack the rig?"

He turned and looked at me, surprised.

"They taught me how at Knoxton. They said everyone should learn how to pack their own."

"That's usually true, but we'll miss the load. And then there's a bunch of students. If you repack, we won't be able to go up for another hour, maybe two. I thought you wanted to go up on the next load?"

I was stuck. I couldn't imagine jumping someone else's pack job. On the other hand, the longer I waited, the greater the chance that something would happen to stop me. I chewed on my lower lip, agonizing.

The phone in the hangar rang, and I whipped my head around. The folding chair was empty and Frank was nowhere to be seen; he must have started his break already.

"Voice mail will get it," Raymond said. "So what do you want to do?"

"Okay," I said. "Let's go."

18

Standard greeting from one skydiver to another:
"Blue skies!"
Standard response:
"Black death!"

—The Whuffo's Guide to Skydiving

When we came out of the hangar, I saw that along with the 182s, Raymond also had a Twin Otter. "An Otter!" I said. Raymond looked at me curiously. "Um, that's what it is, right? I mean, I don't really know . . ."

"Yep, that's what it is. Not many people know one aircraft from another, though."

I shrugged. "I like planes, I guess."

Raymond said, "Cool," and gave me a hand up. The plane didn't have seats, just seat belts bolted into the floor. *It's fine, it's fine*, I told myself. Plenty of jump planes just have seat belts. It's perfectly safe, and it leaves more room for jumpers. Very sensible and economical.

People were climbing in, and Raymond and I scooted farther back. I put my mouth next to his ear so he could hear me over the racket of the engine. "We're going out last?"

"Yup. Why? Want to get it over with?"

I shrugged, trying to look casual.

"Nervous?"

I thought about lying but decided that only an idiot wouldn't be at least a little nervous, so I nodded.

The pilot turned down the runway and accelerated. Raymond handed me an altimeter, and I strapped it onto my wrist. Raymond leaned in close. "Don't worry—do it just like before. I'll be right there if you need me."

I looked out the window. Part of me was saying, *Need you? I won't need you. I don't need anyone.* And part of me was saying, *Like before? There is no "before"! This is crazy—tell him you've changed your mind,* and neither part was drowning out the other. I leaned my forehead against the window and closed my eyes, hoping the shaking would rattle my brain into silence. The sound of the propeller was deafening since the aircraft door had been removed.

I felt the liftoff and opened my eyes again. When we reached a thousand feet, Raymond motioned at me to take off my seat belt. Soon it started feeling cold as we climbed rapidly. I glanced at my altimeter and saw we had passed five thousand feet.

The Missouri landscape spread out below us. The trees were the pale green of early summer, but in a few weeks they would be that heavy, dark color that even looks hot. From this high, everything on the ground seemed clean and whole. The rust spots on the roof of the hangar disappeared and the metal sparkled in the sunlight. The weeds in the cracks in the runway, and even the cracks themselves, were invisible. A car on the road to the DZ looked like one of those little metal toy cars, all cherry-red and shiny and sporty. . . .

I gasped and pressed my forehead to the window again. It couldn't be—but it was. Denny's car was speeding toward the Jump Ranch.

How had he figured out where I'd gone? Well, if he was coming because he thought he could talk me out of it—for one thing he was too late, and for another, it wasn't any of his business. It was nobody's business but mine whether I jumped or not.

A four-way lined up in the door. They took a little while to get into position—it's awkward moving around in such cramped quarters—and finally bombed out. I was in agony. With the delay, the pilot would have to circle around to get me and Raymond out over the right spot. Meanwhile, Denny would recognize my dad's car in the lot. When he didn't find me on the ground, he'd tell someone.

I stared out the window. *Slow down*, I willed Denny. I couldn't see the road, so I moved to the other side of the plane, near the door.

Raymond put out his hand. "Not yet!" he yelled over the prop noise.

"I just want to look out!" I shouted back. Raymond looked puzzled; there were windows all around us to look out of.

But the plane turned on jump run at exactly the wrong time, blocking my view of the road. I glanced at the pilot, wondering when the cut was going to come. He was talking into the microphone on his headset. He turned and looked at me with narrowed eyes.

Vomit rose in my throat.

The pilot's voice came over the crackly intercom. "Ray, I need to speak to you."

Raymond hoisted himself up and leaned over him. The pilot's lips moved and he pointed at me. Raymond turned and now both of them stared at me. Raymond leaned over and asked in my ear, "Is your name Clancy Edwards?" I stared back at him, not knowing whether to admit it or deny it, and then he asked, "Dave Edwards's girl?"

I gulped and nodded. I couldn't read his expression; it looked like anger and fear and maybe embarrassment. He didn't say anything more to me but turned back to the pilot, and I knew he was telling him to land. We started a descent.

Before Raymond could stop me, even before I knew I was going to do it, I hurled myself through the door. Instantly, I thought, *I need to hit rewind*, and then I thought, *You can't rewind real life.*

\\\\\\\\\

The first thing I noticed was the noise. Being in free-fall in the serene-looking sky wasn't any quieter than the plane ride had been—it was louder, if anything. The wind sounded like a freight train when you're too close to the tracks, a pulsing roar that slams your eardrums. I didn't feel like I was falling; I felt like I was the locomotive of that freight train, moving incredibly fast, tumbling every which way, so I didn't even know where the ground was. If I was still tumbling around when I opened, I could get wrapped up in the lines. Didn't happen often, but it was possible. *I have to hit an arch*, I told myself. I flung my arms wide, arched my back, and tried to touch my heels to the back of my head.

Miraculously, the tumbling stopped, and right away the earth rolled smoothly under me like a huge green carpet. The wind still battered my face, forcing my lips back and freezing my teeth. I saw something out of the corner of my eye, and I realized that Ray must have exited right after me and tracked head-down to catch up. He would try to get close, but he needed to avoid flying straight over me. When I pulled I'd come to a near stop, and if he was in freefall above me, we'd slam into each other at more than a hundred miles an hour, and both of us would die.

I didn't know what our exit altitude had been, but it must have been pretty high. Ray would have planned for me to have a long freefall so he could check out whether I could solo. But I didn't want a freefall experience. All I wanted was to open now. I wanted to see a big, bright canopy overhead, to ride it down to the ground to whatever trouble was waiting for me.

I waved off, just in case Ray was over me. I reached to my waist to pull out the pilot chute, but that made me break my arch and I wound up on my back. I hit the arch again and stabled out, but I didn't spend any time enjoying the view. I moved my right arm down, gritting my teeth to force the rest of me to stay in the arch. I found the pilot-chute handle and flung it out.

There came a *thwap* and a tremendous jerk on my upper back, and then the freight-train noise stopped and the sun was warm on my face. I drew in a deep, sobbing breath. I had a canopy above me; all I had to do was steer to the airport and head into the wind and land. It was over.

Only it wasn't.

The ground was still coming up awfully fast and the wind whooshed in my ears, not with the roar of freefall but with a strange whistle. I looked at my altimeter. Although I didn't know how fast my descent rate should be, the needle seemed to be moving faster than made sense. It must be nerves, I told myself, but that couldn't be right. Everyone said that on their first jump the canopy ride felt like the safest, most comfortable thing ever, not like something even more life-threatening than freefall. They also said that it was so slow and smooth that they felt like they were hardly moving. Instead, the ground rushed up at me.

I looked up to check the canopy, and I didn't understand what I was seeing. It should have been a nice, smooth rectangle, but instead, it was a shape that had never existed in any geometry book. What I was looking at, I realized with disbelief that made me want to deny my eyes, was a canopy with a tear down the middle. It had split nearly in half, and the two pieces were hanging together only by the merest strip of fabric.

I fought down the panic that threatened to paralyze me. *What should I do?* All the safety instructions I had overheard while playing with my dolls in the hangar and later while doing my homework, and even later while packing, zipped through my mind. Never had anyone mentioned a canopy ripping partway down the middle. I didn't know if there was enough of it left to land safely, or if it would be better to cut away and dump the reserve.

My helmet didn't have a radio. Okay. I had to figure this out for myself. I looked at the ground between my feet and tried to picture landing at that rate, to determine if I could ride the malfunction in.

I couldn't. Even though I had never been under canopy before, I could tell that I was dropping too fast. I would probably be killed. And I couldn't turn to face into the wind and flare, with the canopy being essentially in two pieces—or could I? I gave one of the steering toggles an experimental tug, and that half of the canopy wrinkled and threatened to collapse.

Holy shit. *When in doubt, whip it out.* I had to cut away. My rate of descent was too fast for a safe landing, but it probably wasn't fast enough to trigger the AAD, and even if the reserve did open, it would risk entanglement with the main.

No. Anything but that.

I had to cut away and open my reserve myself. I tried to concentrate, but everything was too confused. The wind shrilled in my ears and everything swirled around me—the green beneath my feet, the sparkling hangar, the cars, the

Cessnas parked at an angle far below, looking small but getting bigger every second. The ground started filling my field of vision.

And then . . .

It all stopped.

First, the sound clicked off as though someone had hit a "mute" button.

Next, color drained away, and the ground beneath me looked like a black-and-white movie.

And then something on my right shoulder gleamed red, like a stoplight, like a Rudolph nose on a Christmas decoration.

I heard my own voice repeating the words I had listened to my dad and Louisa and Randy and Noel and Leon and every other instructor say, over and over again like a nursery rhyme:

"Look red." I looked down and to my right, at the red cutaway handle that glowed and pulsed until it almost blinded me.

"Hands red." I watched my hands come up and clasp it. *How interesting*, I thought calmly. *Would you look at that*.

"Look silver." My head turned and now I saw my left shoulder, where the silver reserve handle sparkled like a diamond.

"Pull red," said my voice, and although I was fixated on the silver handle so hard that I couldn't see my hands on the red cutaway handle, I felt them yank it, and then I was falling, but it felt weirdly slow and smooth, and there still was no sound of wind.

"Pull silver." I felt the words leave my mouth, and my hands moved across my chest and pulled the silver handle and I was flung around. I gasped, but then the earth rose up and I slammed into something hard, and then I was lying on my side on the ground and all I could hear was my own breathing, and when someone ran up and said, "I think he's alive," I felt a giggle bubble up. I tried to say, "I'm not a he, I'm a she," but all that came out of my mouth was a gush of something hot and wet, and everything went fuzzy, and then black.

\\\\\\\\\\

I came to in the ambulance, or anyway that's what they told me later. I don't remember the ambulance ride or anything else until after the second of my surgeries, when I woke up in a hospital bed sometime in the middle of the night. It was three nights later, I found out afterward. The room was bright and noisy with beeps and clatters, and I had no idea where I was or why I couldn't move or speak. Someone came in and said something, but I didn't understand them, and I fell asleep again.

It turns out that coming out of a coma isn't like in the movies, where you blink and stammer out a few words and then all of a sudden you're back to normal. First of all, I was on a ventilator, so I couldn't talk, and second, everything was very confusing. I wasn't entirely sure where I was or why I was there. My dad sat by my bed and told me I was in the ICU and that I'd had an accident. I vaguely remembered getting into his car and heading out toward town. *I must have crashed*, I thought before I drifted away.

The next time I woke, I was alone. I heard people moving and talking nearby, but nobody seemed to be paying attention to me. I lay there and looked around, moving just my eyes, since my head banged with pain when I tried to turn it. Some pictures were propped up on a counter past my feet: one of my mom running on a beach, and one of my parents right after they were married, and then some of the two of them with me, and one of me and Theo at a party. I wasn't sure why I was in bed and why I didn't want to see the picture of me laughing with Theo. I couldn't move to look away from it, so I closed my eyes.

Someone came in. The footsteps were unfamiliar, and the effort to open my eyes seemed overwhelming, so I didn't try. Then I heard a second person come in, a person with familiar footsteps. It was my dad. I knew that he was going to be angry at me, that I had done something wrong, so I lay still.

"I think she's coming around." It was a female voice.

"How can you tell?" My dad sounded so tired.

"I don't know." A hand stroked my cheek, straightened my sheet, did something to an apparatus above my head. "But when you've been doing this as long as I have, you start recognizing when someone's in there."

A hand took mine. It was large and warm. My dad. My cheeks tickled, and I knew that my own tears were running down them. One pooled in my ear. I felt myself drifting away.

"Clancy?" His voice sounded like it was coming from

a great distance. "C.C.?" The darkness was coming back. "Carys?"

It gave me a little jolt to hear my real name, and the jolt opened my eyes—just for a second, but long enough to see his weary, stubbly face before the darkness swirled over me again.

\\\\\\\\\\

I hung between sleeping and waking, seeing things without knowing if they were real or dreams. Over and over I felt myself drop out of the plane, and sometimes I fell up instead of down, and I swam in the air, frantically trying to feel the pull of gravity, but rising up, up, up into the screamingly bright sun until I melted. Other times my canopy opened and it was fine, a perfect rectangle, but all that lay below my feet was a wide expanse of sea, an ocean with no place to land, and I knew that I would drown. Sometimes I was in freefall and would see a figure flying near me, and it wasn't Raymond but my dad, and I could read my death in his face.

When I could finally tell my dreams from reality, and bits and shreds of memory came back, and when I finally got off the ventilator, my dad and I pieced together what had happened.

When he hadn't seen me for a while that Sunday, he asked Cynthia if she knew where I was. Cynthia said she'd seen me heading to town in his car and thought he'd given me permission to go to the Knoxton Mart, so she didn't say anything at the time. He called my cell. By then, we figured out, I had already arrived at the Jump Ranch and locked my purse, with my phone in it, in the car. My dad went looking for me in the hangar. Denny was sitting on the packing table with a bloody nose, waiting for me to come back from the Mart. Theo had socked him before storming off. My dad called Theo's cell, but he didn't answer because he was driving.

My dad stopped being mad at me for taking his car and got really worried. Denny offered to drive him into town, and my dad took him up on it. They stopped at Adrienne's in case I was there. Melissa was surprised to see my dad because, she told him, she'd seen his car going past, heading west. That was in the opposite direction of home, so my dad couldn't imagine where I had gone.

It was Denny who figured it out. He told my dad that we'd been talking about me doing a skydive at the Jump Ranch, and that maybe I'd decided to do it. My dad said there was no way I would do that, but he couldn't think where else to look, so he and Denny headed there. On the way my dad called and called the manifest desk at the Jump Ranch, but he kept getting their voice mail while Denny drove way too fast for the little country roads. Denny didn't slow down until he slammed on his brakes in the parking lot next to my dad's car, and my dad was running toward bewildered, gray-bearded Frank at the manifest desk before Denny's car even fully stopped.

It took them a few minutes to figure out the connection with Margaret Finnegan's logbook. When Frank described what "Margaret" looked like, my dad knew it was me, and that's when they radioed the pilot.

"So you saw me jump?" I asked.

He nodded, gripping my fingers so tightly that it hurt. I didn't mind. He lowered his face onto our clenched hands, and his shoulders shook.

"I'm sorry," I said softly. I would have touched his head with my other hand, but that arm was in a cast from my wrist almost to my shoulder. I couldn't imagine what that must have felt like, to see my messed-up canopy and then to watch me cut away and go into freefall again, and then see the reserve come out late. "I'm sorry it took me so long to cut away and then so long to dump the reserve."

He raised his head. His face was swollen and red, and his cheeks were wet. "What are you talking about?"

"I know I hesitated a long time. It must have been scary to watch that." I remembered my senses clicking off one by one, allowing me to see and do only what was necessary to save my life without the distraction of noise and color.

He shook his head. "No, C.C., you did everything right. You pulled the steering toggle and when you saw that the canopy wasn't safe, you cut away and pulled the reserve handle smooth as silk. You hit a beautiful arch, just textbook."

"I did?" Was he *proud* of me? "Then why did I get hurt?" I had broken not only my arm but also my leg, my collarbone, and a few ribs—all on the right side, where I guessed I'd landed. I'd punctured a lung and bruised a kidney, and I damaged my spleen so badly that they'd had to remove it.

I'd lost a lot of blood. Plus, I must have banged my head pretty hard to be unconscious for so long.

"Your reserve hesitated before opening. You barely had line stretch on impact."

"Did you see it?"

He nodded. "And, C.C. . . . ."

"What?"

This time I knew what I heard was pride. "You did the best PLF I've ever seen."

19

"Stupid hurts." Definition: unnecessary.
—*The Whuffo's Guide to Skydiving*

They kept me drugged for the pain, and I was stuck in bed for a few days—I don't know exactly how long. But pretty soon the nurses made me get up and walk. I couldn't use crutches because of my collarbone and my arm, so a nurse's aide supported me on either side, and one of them pulled along the IV pole that I was attached to. I fought through the light-headedness enough to make it as far as the bathroom. This meant one less bedpan, which made me even happier than it made the nurse's aide who would have had to empty it. I was so exhausted that I fell asleep as soon as I was back in bed.

When I woke up to see Angie by the side of my bed, reading a magazine, I was sure it was another dream. But she glanced around and saw me looking at her. She stood and kissed me on the cheek.

"Is Jackson making another jump?" I asked.

She shook her head. "I'm here just for you, baby."

"Leanne doesn't need you?"

"Leanne will be okay. My other girl needs me more now."

It took me a minute to realize she meant me.

"Besides, the nurses were threatening to go on strike if Dave didn't go home and take a shower. He told them I was your aunt, and to prove it I rattled off your birthday and cell number. I could have told them your Social Security number too, but they believed me. They said I could hang out here and let him go home and clean up. I hope he's also taking a nap."

"How is he?" I asked after a moment.

"Better. It was pretty bad at first. You lost a lot of blood when you ruptured your spleen, and they had to give you a transfusion. Dave tried to be the blood donor and when they told him he was the wrong type, I thought he'd lose it for sure."

"He thinks he can fix anything," I said, and Angie grunted in agreement.

"The doctor told me you can be perfectly fine without a spleen," I said after a pause.

"I've never understood why we have one, then," Angie said.

I closed my eyes. Conversation was exhausting. "What did my dad say about my accident?"

"Not much." Not surprising. "But Denny said—"

My eyes popped open. "You saw Denny?"

"No, talked to him. He drove your dad here and called me from outside the emergency room. Your dad told the cops to give him my number from your cell."

"What did he say about what happened?"

"He said Dave ran so fast to where you landed that Denny couldn't keep up, and during the whole drive to the hospital, he would cuss for a while and say he was so mad at you he couldn't see straight, and then he'd get all quiet and moan and—"

"Stop it." I covered my face with my good hand. Him cussing and being mad at me I could take; picturing him quiet and moaning was unbearable. For the first time I was glad that I'd been out of it for so long that by the time I was conscious, he had gotten over the worst of the shock.

Angie tucked a tissue between my fingers. I wiped my eyes and blew my nose. "Have you talked to Denny again, after that?" I asked.

"Nope. You heard from him?"

I shook my head.

"From Theo?"

"No phone or Wi-Fi where he is. He probably doesn't even know."

"Hm."

It wasn't like Angie not to say what she was thinking, so I looked at her. "What?" I asked.

"Talk to your dad about that," she said. "In fact, it's time you and your dad talked about a lot of things."

"Like what?"

"Like your mom."

I sat up even though the room spun around me. "He won't talk to me about her—he never has. Never will. It's like she's his own special property, nothing to do with me." I flopped back on the pillow as little lights danced around me.

Angie grabbed the control box attached to my bed and pushed some buttons, lowering my head and raising my feet. "Want me to call the nurse?" she asked.

I started to shake my head but the room swirled around me again, so I closed my eyes and said, "No, just some water." I felt the straw touch my lips and took a sip. I opened my eyes. Angie was right there.

"I shouldn't have upset you," she said, squeezing my hand. "To be fair, it's not really up to you to start the conversation. Dave's the grown-up here; he should be the one telling you things you need to know. But if he won't, maybe you should start."

"What do you mean, things I need to know?" I asked hoarsely. My eyelids felt heavy. Angie stroked my face, and my eyes closed again.

"Ask your dad," she said. "You two need to talk more. You're too tired now anyway, and I have to get back to Leanne. I'm leaving early tomorrow morning." I felt her lips brush my forehead in a good-bye kiss.

I must have fallen asleep, because when I opened my eyes, it was dark, Angie was gone, and my dad was reading in the chair next to my bed. I thought about what Angie had said to me, but I didn't know what to say to him. So I didn't say anything.

The next day Elise came with a new nightgown that looked enough like a dress that I could wear it when I had visitors, and she had packed my makeup, my phone charger, and a few other things.

"I know you're tired, so I won't stay long," she said, still standing, as I shook out the nightgown one-handed. It was nice; she hadn't made the mistake of buying me something pink with lace and rosebuds. "I just thought it might not have occurred to Dave that you'd need all this." She gestured at the makeup and the tampons.

"Thanks," I said. I reached my good arm out to her and she leaned in and gave me a hug. Then she said she was late for work and left.

I had a few visitors—they wouldn't let in too many at a time—but Theo didn't come. The day after Elise's visit, I asked my dad if Theo knew what had happened, like Angie had said I should. If it went well, maybe I'd get brave enough to ask him about my mom.

He nodded. "He had to go back to camp. He wanted to visit, but I was the only one allowed in the ICU, so I convinced him to wait until you were in a regular room. And then right before they moved you, he had to go back to camp to take some kids on a hike. He sent those." He pointed at the purple and yellow flowers that were wilting on the windowsill.

So Theo knew how badly I was hurt, and he couldn't even take an afternoon off to go into town where he could call me. Funny—I didn't feel sad about that. Just kind of resigned.

I still didn't want to talk to my dad about my mom, though. It would be weird, after so many years of hardly mentioning her, to bring her up out of the blue. It wasn't that I was chicken—or so I told myself.

Later that day I was channel surfing and my dad said, "You know, Denny did his solo."

I looked up from the remote in surprise. "He did? When?"

"Last weekend. I thought he'd back out after he saw you almost . . . after he saw your accident, but he finished up student status the next Saturday and did his solo on Sunday."

"How'd he do?"

"Great. No problems, and he stood it up. He didn't have a videographer for this one—said he wanted to be all alone up there. But Mad Jack filmed him from the ground so Denny could show his friend. It's online. You want your laptop?"

I shook my head. The longer I stayed offline, the longer I could wait to reenter the real world, where I'd have to apologize to people and explain what had happened. My phone battery had died, and I didn't tell my dad to plug it into the charger. I didn't want to see what Theo had written to me, or Denny either.

"Did Denny buy a case of beer?" I asked.

"Well, Randy left for a while and came back with a case that afternoon, and I have a feeling some money changed hands, but I didn't ask."

"Dad?"

"Hmm?" The sleepy sound of his voice made me drowsy too.

"Did something—what happened to the Jump Ranch?"

"What do you mean?"

"Did they get into trouble?"

"Damn right they did. They were breaking all sorts of regulations. They've been closed down."

"Oh no," I protested. "It was my fault, not theirs!"

He said firmly, "You're a minor, and they were culpable. And it's not just you, C.C. The place was a mess. It's a miracle no one's been killed there."

"But Raymond was so nice!"

"I know. He's a nice guy. Sloppy, but nice. But honey, there's a reason for those regulations. It's okay now; they're out of business. Our insurance company is suing—"

"But it wasn't his fault! I don't want to sue him for something *I* did!"

He raised his hand. "It's not up to you, C.C.; it's not even up to me. There's no reason our insurance company should have to pay for someone else's negligence."

"They weren't negligent! I had that logbook—"

"I know. Margaret Finnegan's." Dad's voice was grim. "They should have asked you for ID. They should have run over safety procedures with you since Margaret's last jump was so long ago. And most of all, they shouldn't have allowed that canopy to be used. The feds impounded it, so I can't inspect it, but it was obviously worn out. I would have shredded it long ago rather than risk someone's life with it. Plus, the pack job on the reserve—"

"Okay, okay." I lay back on my pillows, feeling dizzy. "It's still my fault."

"It's not your fault that they're closed down. They were an accident waiting to happen. What *is* your fault is that you're hurt, and that you scared the shit out of me." My dad cussed so rarely that it shocked the dizziness from my head. He went on more calmly. "Shutting them down probably saved another jumper's life. Someone was going to get killed there—someone who didn't know what they were doing." Hearing my dad almost say that I knew what I was doing made me feel a little better.

I said, "But Dad, people will think you ran him out of business because he was competition!"

"Sweetie, I don't care what people think, and anyway, I had nothing to do with it. The feds closed him down while I was here with you. He'll probably have to sell his aircraft to pay the fines."

I pondered that for a minute. "You should buy the Otter. It's sweet."

He laughed. "I don't know any other sixteen-year-old girl who'd have an opinion about a Twin Otter, especially while she was lying in a hospital bed all busted up! Anyway, I have my eye on one of the Cessnas. Norton says it's the best aircraft there."

I stretched my fingers like the physical therapist had been bugging me to do. It hurt, but not as much as the day before. I carefully kept from looking at my dad and asked, "Did he jump again after his solo?"

"Who, Denny?"

I nodded.

"He was supposed to—Cynthia put him on a load and he was going to try a kiss pass with Buddy, but right before they were supposed to go up, I saw him run into the office and then out to the parking lot. He got in his car and peeled out. Cynthia said he never canceled his jump, but he didn't come back either."

"And you don't know what the call was about?"

My dad shook his head.

It had to be Frederick. Should I call Denny? Or at least text? I hesitated. He must have been angry that I'd lied about my age and hadn't told him about Theo, and he'd say things that hurt all the more because they were true. Or he'd be cold and tell me it had been fun knowing me, he was sorry I was hurt, and he'd see me around. I didn't know which would be worse.

I tried to watch a movie but couldn't get interested in it. I felt too guilty, both about the Jump Ranch and about what all this had to be costing my dad. It was good that Skydive Knoxton would be getting more business, what with the Jump Ranch being out of the picture. I didn't know much about insurance, but I was sure there would be lots of bills from my surgeries and rehab, and they probably wouldn't all be covered. I'd already decided that I was going to turn my bank account and my cashbox over to my dad to help pay them. It wasn't much, but it was the best I could do, and I hoped it would make a difference.

It would definitely make a difference to my plans to leave home for school. I wouldn't have the money I'd been counting on, and I'd missed too many summer-school classes to get the AP credits I needed to give me a head start on my double major. *Stupid. I should forget about archaeology and major in something practical, like business or engineering.*

I kept stretching my fingers. When I next glanced at my dad he was asleep, his head back against the chair. He'd start snoring soon.

I could just reach my laptop. I powered it up, using the earbuds from my iPod so I wouldn't wake my dad, and found the video. Denny walked across the landing area and didn't seem to notice Mad Jack filming him as he climbed into the Caravan. The next shot started when the plane, high up and small, turned on jump run. The engine cut, and then a dot appeared in the sky. "He's out," Louisa said. Jack, still on the ground, zoomed in on Denny, and you could make out his arms and legs. Denny did two 360s, and then a back loop, and then another one. He waved off and tossed out the pilot chute. The blue-and-white canopy opened, and I wondered who was packing while I was in the hospital.

Jack filmed a little of Denny's canopy ride and then the landing, where Denny flared a bit too low and tripped after he hit the ground. He bounced right to his feet, though, and as he gathered up the lines and the canopy carefully to make the pack job easier for whoever had taken my place in the hangar, I blinked back tears. I was so weak that even seeing puppies in a commercial made me want to cry, much less watching Denny do a near-perfect solo.

I realized that I had never told anyone from the online

school what had happened, and sure enough, there were emails about missing tests and assignments. I was about to write back to the instructor to explain that I'd had an accident when I saw an email from Denny.

I closed my email, opened it again, closed it again, and then muttered to myself, "This is stupid," and read his message.

> Hey Clancy, hope you're doing better. I wanted to text but your phone goes to voice mail so I don't know if it got smashed in the jump. Sorry I left without coming to see you in the hospital but Frederick got really sick with a fungal infection and I had to go.

That was all. I couldn't get out of bed to plug my phone in, and I certainly didn't want to wake up my dad, so I hit "reply" and wrote slowly, painfully with my left hand, which had IV needles stuck in it:

> doing ok. sort of. out of icu. how's f?

I didn't have to wait long for his answer.

> Passed away on Monday. Funeral was today. I gave the eulogy. Advice: don't ever eulogize your best friend. It sucks so bad.

I started typing one-handed but gave up in frustration. I

pushed back the covers and sat up, despite a rush of wooziness, so I could reach the drawer of the bedside table, where my dad had left my phone and charger.

"What are you doing, young lady?"

Dad was awake. My face must have told him that something was bad wrong, because in a flash his arm was around me, holding me up as I shook. "What is it? Clancy, what's wrong? Does something hurt?"

I said in a rush, "Denny's best friend died and I have to talk to him and my battery's dead—" A sob tore at my throat at the word.

"Okay, sweetie, okay. Lie back down. I'll plug it in." He handed me the phone. "Good?"

I nodded, trying to breathe evenly, looking for Denny's call. The last thing he needed was for me to cry.

"I'll just leave, then," my dad said, showing a tact I didn't know he had. "Tell him I'm sorry about his friend."

Denny's phone rang only once. "Clancy?" His voice was hoarse.

"Denny," I said as the tears fell. "Denny. I'm sorry. I'm so, so sorry." And although at first I meant I was sorry about Frederick, I really meant I was sorry about everything.

20

"**H**ang on for speed bumps," the orderly said as the automatic doors slid open, and I got my first breath of fresh air in what seemed like months instead of weeks. The fact that it was muggy, humidity-laden air under a dull, gray sky was irrelevant. It was free of hospital smell and beeping machines and people waking me up to ask about bowel movements. My dad trailed behind, carrying two shopping bags with my things in them, including pain pills and elastic bands for exercises to strengthen my leg when it came out of the cast, and rubber balls to squeeze to keep my arm muscles from getting flabby. I held the strings of a bouquet of helium balloons—now semideflated—that had come from the Geezers, a stuffed skydiving monkey from Angie, and a card that everyone at the DZ had signed.

The orderly stopped at the curb while my dad trotted ahead to get the car. I don't know which of us was more eager to get me out of there. They both helped me into the backseat, and the orderly showed my dad how to buckle me in so that the chest strap part of the seat belt wouldn't press on my collarbone. He told me to lean forward and put a small pillow behind me.

My dad pulled into the circular drive so slowly that a pregnant woman on the sidewalk, leading a toddler by the hand, passed us. We inched into the street. "You okay back there?" he asked.

"Fine. Great." I looked at people going about their business, little kids running ahead of their parents, traffic lights blinking from yellow to red. I had never realized before how beautiful the city was, even on a soggy, gray summer day like this one. My dad looked at me in the rearview mirror, and I could tell from the crinkles around his eyes that he was smiling.

"What?" I asked.

"Reminds me of the other time I brought you home from the hospital. When you were two days old. You were in a car seat in the back and your mom sat next to you, and I cringed at every little bump or short stop until she got mad and told me that you weren't going to break. She said if I treated you like a piece of glass, you'd wind up believing it."

"Huh." I had never heard that story.

He looked at me again, and this time his eyes weren't smiling. "I'm sorry, C.C."

"*You're* sorry? I'm the one who messed up!"

"Oh, you sure did. You're right about that. You messed up big-time. But I think I'm at least partially responsible."

"You? What did *you* do?"

He didn't answer, acting like negotiating a curve was taking all his concentration. But I could tell he was stalling. The road straightened out, and he said carefully, "I think your mom was right—I've been making you think you're fragile. I kind of wonder if that's why you felt you had to bust out so dramatically."

Well, hallelujah, I thought but didn't say. I was afraid that if I spoke, he'd stop.

"I couldn't bear the thought of you getting hurt. By anything. By anyone. I felt my job was to protect you."

"And look what happened."

"Exactly." I thought that was the end of it. It was about the longest conversation of this kind we'd ever had. To my surprise, he continued. "If you had . . . C.C., if you'd gone in, I could never have lived with the guilt. Never. I've never gotten over feeling guilty about your mom, and—"

"Wait a second," I interrupted him. I forced myself to take a deep breath. "*You* feel guilty about Mom? Why? You didn't pack her rig, did you?"

"Oh no, nothing as simple as that."

I waited.

"The thing is, she was distracted that day. She couldn't

have been in the right frame of mind to jump. And that was my fault."

"How was that your fault?" I asked.

The words came gushing out of him so fast I could hardly keep up. "I never told you this. I didn't want you to know. But I think you need to know it now. The night before Jenna went in, I told her I was leaving her. I told her I was taking you and going someplace to start over. I said we never should have gotten married, we were too different and I was too old for her, and now it was catching up with us. I had thought that once you were born she'd calm down, but she was just so . . . so wild. She'd disappear for days and not tell me where she'd been, and she was drinking before jumping—not just a beer, which would have been bad enough, but she'd drink hard liquor all afternoon and then make a sunset jump."

I couldn't process what he was saying. *My mom did that?* "Dad—you're not saying—you don't think she did it on purpose because of what you said, do you? Because—"

"Oh no, sweetie. I saw her; she tried everything possible to save herself. She just waited too long. She cut away too late. AADs weren't as accurate then as they are now. She should have made up her mind to cut away earlier. I'm not saying that she meant to die."

"Then are you saying she was drunk when she went in?" The thought horrified me.

He shook his head. "She wouldn't drink before an important practice. And toxicology came back negative. Thank God. I don't think I could have stood that."

"You had her tested?"

"The insurance company did. No, I mean just what I said. I think she was distracted. She probably didn't sleep well after our fight, and during the jump she was thinking about what I had said and about the possibility of losing you, not about the right way to deal with her malfunction."

"Were you really going to leave her?" I couldn't absorb this. It was all too new.

He pulled over to the side of the road, turned off the engine, and twisted around to face me. His eyes were red. He nodded.

"And you were going to take me with you?"

"I couldn't stand to leave you," he said. "And anyway, I didn't think she was good for you. But maybe I was wrong. She loved you, I know that, and you loved her so much. Maybe you would have done better with her than with me." He was crying, and then I was crying too. I wanted to hug him, but as busted up as I was, it would have hurt too much, and besides, his seat was between us.

"I wouldn't have done better with anyone else." I meant it. "But Dad, why didn't you tell me this before?"

"You never want to talk about your mom. I've been respecting that. Angie said to give you space, and—"

"I thought *you* were the one who didn't want to talk about her!"

His smile was sad. "I didn't—I don't, not with anyone else. But with you, it's different. You should know about her. And anyway, right before Angie left, she said it was time you knew. She was right, wasn't she?"

I nodded, unable to speak.

He reached back and wiped the tears off my cheeks. "Can I ask you one thing?" I nodded again. "When you were up there—when you cut away and dumped the reserve, and then when you did your PLF—did you see her? Did you hear her? Did she help you?"

I wrestled with myself. I thought I knew what he wanted to hear, what he wanted me to say, but I couldn't do it. I just couldn't lie about this. It was too important. Besides, it was time we started telling each other the truth. "No," I finally said. "I was alone. It was all me." I thought he'd be disappointed, but I was wrong.

"That's my girl." A grin shone on his teary face. He turned the car back on and pulled into the street.

When we stopped at the house, the first thing I saw was a big banner stretching across the porch saying **WELCOME HOME CLANCY**. The second thing I saw was Julia standing under it, and behind her were Justin and Cory and some other people. Julia and Cory had visited me in the hospital a couple times, but my dad hadn't let anyone else come. "Teenagers are too germy," he'd said.

My dad got the rented wheelchair out of the trunk and settled me into it. Justin helped him haul the chair up the porch steps. Each step jolted me, and I had to bite my lower lip to keep from yelping.

When I rolled into the den, Julia ran to give me a hug, but my dad said, "Careful! Broken girl here!" and she stopped. She and Cory were used to what I looked like, but the others stared at me, various degrees of dismay on their faces.

I knew what they were seeing. I was pale and thin, my makeup was all weird from being put on one-handed, I still had a bruise on the side of my face, and there was a cast from my upper arm almost to my fingertips and another one on my right leg. At least they couldn't see the scar where my spleen used to be.

"Welcome home," Nicole said uncertainly. I spotted a sheet cake on the table and decorations in the den.

My dad leaned down and asked quietly, "Want me to get rid of them?" I nodded, and he said, "Sorry, kids, she has to lie down. Julia, take that cake, and all of you have a celebration someplace else. She'll let you know when she's ready for company."

"Thanks for coming," I called to them, waving apologetically as my dad wheeled me through the den. He helped me into the big hospital bed that nearly filled my bedroom and put the side up. "I'm not going to fall out," I told him.

"Doctor's orders." He kissed my forehead and smoothed the hair off my face. "Get some rest. You let me know when you need me."

"'Kay," I said. I closed my eyes and heard him leave. I was exhausted, but I wasn't sleepy. I felt like I'd slept enough in the hospital to last me the rest of my life.

Voices were murmuring somewhere not far off. I called, "Dad?"

He came in. "Did we wake you?"

I shook my head. "Who are you talking to? One of the doctors?"

He glanced out the door. "Denny. He drove in from

Denver last night to pack up his apartment, and he wants to see you."

"It's okay," I said, trying not to show that my heart was racing. "He can come in."

My dad went out again and then Denny was there. He couldn't hide his shock at my beat-up appearance any better than the others could.

I found the bed controls—I'd become an expert—and pushed the button that made me sit up. Denny picked up my good hand and sat down gingerly on the edge of the bed.

"I won't break," I assured him.

"Promise?" His voice was husky.

"Denny, I—" I began, but he stopped me.

"It's okay. I know you're sorry, and I know you'll be okay. I can't stay long—I shouldn't have come at all, but I just had to see you to make sure you were really in one piece."

"Are you moving to a different apartment? My dad said you were packing up your—"

"I'm going back to Denver."

"You're *what*?" I sat up straighter and then collapsed back on the pillow. I took a breath and tried to sound calm as I asked, "Why? It's not because of me, is it?"

He shook his head. "I've decided to stay home for a while. Frederick's brother is having a really hard time and his mom thinks I can help. Even if I can't, I'm not really in the right frame of mind to start college yet. I've deferred Clemens until January."

Outside the door my dad cleared his throat. Denny stood. "Okay if I call once in a while?" He gestured at my right arm, still immobilized in its cast. "Doesn't look like you can text too well."

I reached up my good hand and touched his cheek. His golden eyes suddenly had tears in them. "Call whenever you like," I whispered just before he pressed a soft kiss on my lips. And then he was gone.

\\\\\\\\\\

A month later, Julia and I stared up at the steps leading to the front door of the high school. I swear I could feel my dad watching us, just out of sight.

"Wow," Julia said finally. "I never realized how many stairs there were."

"Me neither." It wasn't that long a staircase, really, just three sets of four steps each, with a handicapped ramp off to the right. But I refused to start junior year in a wheelchair—or worse, using one of those old-lady walkers with tennis balls on the ends of its legs. Or even with my dad helping me. I'd thought I'd be out of the cast by the first day of school, but they'd had to rebreak my leg and set it again, and I was still getting used to crutches.

I handed one of them to Julia and took hold of the banister with my left hand. I swung the crutch around and hoisted myself up. The first-day crowd had thinned, since final bell was about to ring. Both Julia and I had permission to arrive late today as I figured out how to do this. My dad had told the principal that it would be easier for me to navigate the stairs without the usual throng, and that was true, but I also wanted to be late enough to make sure that I wouldn't run into Mr.-Perfect-Attendance-Never-Even-Had-A-Tardy Theo.

First set of steps done.

I swung the crutch again. I got tired easily after spending the second half of the summer propped up on the couch with a book when I wasn't at physical therapy, so I went more slowly up the second bunch of steps. I was glad when my phone chirped and gave me an excuse to stop.

"Better turn that off before you get inside," Julia reminded me.

I couldn't help smiling as I read the text. Julia asked me a question with her eyes.

"Denny," I said.

"Ah."

She was obviously about to burst with curiosity, so I took pity on her. "He got a job at the Denver Zoo."

"Doing what?"

"Doesn't know yet. He hopes it's not in the monkey house."

I was about to tackle the second set of steps when Julia said under her breath, "Scumbag alert."

I looked up and saw Theo standing at the top of the stairs. Julia moved aside and pretended to be interested in something on her phone as he came down to me. I would be friendly, I had resolved earlier—friendly but impersonal.

"Hey." He sounded shy.

"Hey." I wasn't about to help him out.

He shifted from one foot to the other and squinted into

the sun. He'd gotten his hair cut short, and with his dark chin stubble, he looked good. I glanced at the next set of steps, wondering if I'd rested long enough to tackle them, and realized that I didn't care how good Theo looked. It was like seeing a picture of a guy in a magazine, thinking, "Hot," and turning the page.

"Need any help?"

"No, thanks. Julia's got it. And we're about to be late. Mr. Norris only gave me fifteen extra minutes." He didn't move, and I lifted my crutch so I could get to the bottom step of the final set of stairs. "'Scuse me," I said, but he stayed put.

"I'm sorry," he whispered, and then a bit louder, "I didn't know what you were planning. I would have stopped you." I clamped my teeth shut on my retort. "That girl—Ali—she doesn't mean anything to me. It was just a summer thing. If I'd known it was going to upset you so much that you'd jump out of a plane to get back at me, I'd never—"

"*What?*" Breaking my resolve to stay cool and distant, I looked up at him. The sight of his puppy-dog eyes suddenly infuriated me. "You think I jumped to get back at you?"

"I know you went out with that guy to make me jealous," he went on as though I hadn't spoken. "That's why you took him to Manuelito's, so I'd be sure to hear about it. And I didn't mean for you to see the picture of me and Ali rock climbing. I can't believe you'd go all the way to making a jump, though."

"And you thought all of that was because of *you*?" I burst out. "I took Denny to Manuelito's to make you jealous, and I jumped out of an airplane to get back at you? Okay, maybe what you told me made me realize some things about myself, about how I've been letting you and my dad make decisions for me, but that's all. None of this has anything to do with you. It has to do with me, just with *me*! Do you think you're so—"

Julia moved closer, all pretense of checking her phone forgotten. "Clancy." She put a hand on my arm.

I shook it off. "When I need someone to help me, I'll ask for it, like I asked Julia today. But we're going to be late now, so *back off*."

Tears streamed down my face as I swung myself up the steps, fueled by adrenaline. Julia held the door open and together we made our way down the hall to our first-period class. As we slid into our seats—well, she slid, I kind of sideways-hopped—Señora Richardson said, "*Bienvenidas, Julia y Clancy*," and we answered, "*Buenos días.*"

It was like none of it had happened.

Here we were back in Señora Richardson's classroom, with the map of Latin America on one wall and Spain on another, just like last year. The smell of the whiteboard markers was the same, the sound of Señora Richardson's voice was the same, we were even sitting in the same seats we'd had sophomore year. When I didn't think about my scars and my missing spleen and the big cast on my leg, the summer was already a memory.

But it wasn't all the same. My dad and I were feeling out our new relationship. Theo and I were history. I had nearly killed myself, and I had met a boy I really liked who didn't try to protect me from the big, bad world.

I realized that everyone was looking at me. "What?" I hastily corrected it to "*¿Qué?*"

"Everyone has to say what they did this summer," Julia stage-whispered.

My heart was still pounding from my encounter with Theo, and the tears must have still been visible on my cheeks, but a giggle rose in my chest at the thought of trying to explain my summer, let alone in Spanish, and then Julia sputtered, and before I knew it we were both laughing like lunatics.

I didn't know whether I'd see Denny when he came back. I hoped so, but I had some work to do if I wanted him to trust me again. I also didn't know if my dad would ever learn to let go, really let go, and I didn't know if I'd ever be able to see Theo in the school halls without wanting to scream at him.

What I did know was that from now on I'd be in charge of my own life—the good parts and the bad parts—and if things didn't work out the way I planned, I'd pull my own reserve and land on my own two feet. One foot and one cast, actually. That thought struck me as funny, for some reason, and I snorted a laugh again.

"Clancy?" Señora Richardson sounded worried, and I managed to pull myself together.

"Carys," I said on impulse. "*Me llamo Carys.*"

"Carys." She looked puzzled but nodded, and I tried to put together a few verbs and nouns to say that over the summer I had worked for my dad and had had an accident, but that I was okay. She corrected my mistakes and moved on to the next person, and junior year officially started.

21

FACT: Every year in the United States, people jump out of airplanes about two million times.

—*The Whuffo's Guide to Skydiving*

"Almost there!" Norton's voice was barely audible over the roar of the engine that blasted through the Cessna's open door. It didn't matter if I heard him, though; Norton knew that I was aware of our altitude. I think he just wanted to treat me like any other first-jump student.

I had been eighteen for three days and hadn't made a jump yet. I'd had a history final on my actual birthday, which was a Friday, and then it had poured all day on Saturday. Sunday morning it was still drizzling, but late in the afternoon the clouds had thinned, and my dad said it was okay to go for it. Norton already had the engine revving when I came running out of the hangar, all rigged up, so that we could get to altitude before the sun set, which would force us to land before I could get out.

It was just like an observer ride, except that I was wearing not one but two parachutes—the main and the reserve. I was squashed into the back with Jonathan—aka "the Geezer with the big gray eighties mustache," the one who had put my mom out on her first jump. Norton had taken us up fast, and now we were turning onto jump run.

The big difference between this and an observer ride was that the next time the engine cut, it would be me who was getting out, not some other jumper. Aside from Norton, no one else was in the plane but Jonathan, and he was going to stay in and observe me from inside. I'd be alone in the sky, with no videographer, no AFF instructor—just me. I couldn't tell if the massive butterflies pounding my stomach meant I was afraid or excited or what. I just knew that if I didn't get out soon, I'd fizzle over.

My dad was on the ground, along with most of Skydive Knoxton's regulars, as well as Julia and Cory. Cory was Julia's new boyfriend, which was weird for me, but a huge improvement over Justin. Angie had come home from her daughter's house for good almost a year before and now she was down there with Patsy and the others, all of them in their SkyWitches costumes. Denny was trying to get out of his shift in the lab so he could be there, but since the experiment was about to wrap up, he didn't know if his professor would let him. One of my new friends from the community college where I was doing the prerequisites for my archaeology major was there too, which was nice.

Jonathan hooked the static line to the ripcord on my back and patted me on the shoulder to tell me to scoot to the door. The engine cut, and before Jonathan had a chance to say, "Climb out," I was on my feet—I had to crouch, because the roof was so low—and stood, hunched over, in the open door. I pulled the goggles down over my eyes and ran over the procedure in my mind. When there's a wheel right under the door, you can't just bomb out or you'll hit it. You have to remind the pilot to lock the wheel so it won't spin, climb out onto it, hold on to the wing strut, kick your feet up, and let go.

I leaned in close to Norton and said, "Lock the wheel," because I had to, not because I thought he'd forget. He gave me a thumbs-up and blew me a kiss.

The cold, damp wind slammed into me as I leaned out the door. A glimpse of a cherry-red car pulling into the lot next to the hangar almost made me smile and calmed the butterflies a bit.

The sleeves of my jumpsuit fluttered madly, as did a strand of hair that had come untucked. It whipped my face and stung, but I didn't shove it back under my helmet. If I took too long getting out, I'd have to wait in the doorway while we made another circle so that I'd exit at the right spot, and I didn't know if I could stand another circle. I wanted out *now*.

I wrapped my hands around the wing strut that ran diagonally upward from the fuselage to the wing and pulled myself out, stepping on the wheel first with my right foot and then with my left. I slid my hands as far up the strut as they would reach and looked back in the door of the plane, fighting the wind that was trying to knock me off, seeing the static line stretch back through the door. *Like a giant umbilical cord*, I had the time to think before Jonathan hollered, "Go!" The wind whipped most of the word back into the plane, and I kicked up my feet and arched my back and let go.

I flew.

Acknowledgments

I started *Freefall Summer* during the 2012 National Novel Writing Month (www.NaNoWriMo.org) challenge, at the end of which a messy, bloated version of this story (then called *The Icarus Complex*) emerged.

Grateful thanks to my editor, Monica Perez, who saw the potential in the story and helped mold it into what it is now. As always, deep thanks to my agent, Lara Perkins, whose advice and support have been invaluable, and who has always been Clancy's biggest cheerleader.

Much gratitude to the late Mark Curto, who read and commented on the manuscript in an early stage. Many thanks to Jan Works, who offered important suggestions for changes to both the writing and the details of skydiving, and to Pat Works, whose encyclopedic knowledge of the history of the sport was very helpful.

My gratitude to Dr. Sheila McMorrow-Jones (Emergency Medicine, Pediatrics) at Vanderbilt University Medical Center for her careful reading of the medical portions of this book. Any errors that slipped in after her reading are, of course, my own responsibility.

Many thanks to Bob Hawkins, who more or less dared me to take a first-jump course (which he taught) and who then put me out on my first jump and many subsequent jumps, including my last freefall, when I landed in the middle of the Cribari vineyard (thanks a lot for that spot, Hawk!). Thanks to Jonathan Manheim, who introduced me to skydiving and who graciously allowed me to use his Para-Commander after I graduated from a round canopy.

One day when I was having trouble packing that Para-Commander (the spring-loaded pilot chute kept popping out and smacking me in the face), a six-foot-seven-inch man with a pronounced southern accent offered to help. I accepted gratefully. Not the usual way to meet the love of your life, but thirty-something years and two children later, I'm happy to claim it. Thank you for helping me save my own life those many years ago, and for every year since then, Greg.